UNDERCOVER WITH THE RANCHER

BARB HAN

TORJAKE PUBLISHING

To my family for unwavering love and support. I can't imagine doing life with anyone else. I love you guys with all my heart.

"Whatever it is, I won't do it." Romy Nelson tightened her grip on the pencil she'd been holding as she sat at her kitchen table, nursing a cup of coffee as she spoke to her younger sister on the phone.

"I haven't asked for anything yet." Sasha's protest fell on deaf ears.

"You don't have to. I know that tone of voice," Romy said. She couldn't count the number of times she'd bailed her younger half-sister out of trouble—trouble that was growing bigger each time. Last year ago, Romy had practically emptied her savings to pay several months of Sasha's rent after she'd 'lost' her job. Turned out, Sasha had walked off halfway through her shift because she got into a fight with the cook. She still swore he'd overcooked her orders on purpose so that she'd get lousy tips. Romy later found out Sasha had been more than a little economical with the truth, and it wasn't so much that he overcooked her orders that their personalities clashed.

The line was quiet. Too quiet. It meant Sasha was

regrouping and would come at Romy from a fresh angle. She was a master at figuring out the one button to push that caused Romy to cave. This time, she would stay strong. Sasha needed to learn to live with the consequences of her actions; she was twenty years old, not a kid anymore. She was smart and determined when she really put her mind to something, but her past always seemed to get to her, shutting her down the minute Sasha started making progress. She would do something to sabotage her success, and Romy would come to the rescue.

"Hey, listen, I do need your help but it's different this time. Really different." Sasha came clean. Panic gripped Romy at the hint of desperation in her half-sister's voice. Romy squeezed the pencil a little tighter, tapping the eraser against the wood table. The voice on the other end of the phone lowered, and said "It's big, Romy. I'm in real trouble this time."

"How bad can it be?" Romy was probably going to regret asking the question, and yet she couldn't help but feel responsible for Sasha after the abuse she'd suffered at the hands of her mother and the many 'uncles' she brought home. Sasha had been a child support check to her mother, and not much more. "I'm out of money, so—"

Sasha sucked in a breath; the telltale sign she was about to cry. This was so not going to be good.

"I'm having an affair with..." Sasha stopped like she needed a minute before she could reveal the name. The move didn't bode well.

"Break it off," Romy countered.

"That's not the problem," Sasha said, sounding like she was afraid to breathe. She was a good kid at heart, always had been despite the crummy circumstances she'd been dealt. Romy had made a promise she couldn't keep. One that said she'd keep Sasha safe. To be fair, Romy had had no idea how bad it had become at Sasha's childhood house, but she should've. Looking back, the long sleeve shirts in summer should have raised a red flag. Romy had been too caught up in her own world to notice and now she was filled with nothing but regret for not catching on sooner.

"Then, you're going to have to do a better job of explaining this to me, Sasha." Romy set the pencil down before she cracked it in half.

"All I need you to do is work at a ranch and bring back information," Sasha said, like spying on a ranch was no big deal.

"No," she said without hesitation.

"Please," Sasha continued. "You have no idea how badly I need this."

"I can't do this," Romy stated, hating the desperation in her half-sister's voice.

"I shouldn't have called you. I just thought that maybe you'd be able to help." The disappointment and fear in Sasha's voice set the hair on the back of Romy's neck to standing.

There was no way she should let herself get sucked into more of Sasha's drama, especially while Romy was trying to figure out her own next step in life. And yet, she'd never quite been able to bring herself to completely refuse.

"What ranch? And what kind of information?" Romy didn't like any of this, but it didn't sound like the worse thing she'd ever been asked to do. Immoral? Yes. Illegal? Had to be. She would get her half-sister to talk and then help her see this couldn't possibly be the answer.

"About the family's business dealings and a will. I guess someone died and there's a secret stipulation. My contact wants to know what it is," Sasha said, a spark of hope in her voice. "It can't be all that bad, right? I would never bring you into this if there was another way, Romy. You have to know that."

The guilt trip struck a nerve.

"I don't hear from you for months. You don't answer my calls or texts, and now you call out of the blue asking me to spy on random people I've never met?" Romy asked. Her sister had to realize this wasn't something Romy would ever feel comfortable with. Loaning Sasha money that would never come back had been bad enough, but at least it wasn't illegal.

"I'm being blackmailed, Romy."

"Even so, I won't do it. I won't spy on innocent people to get you out of trouble. We'll figure out another way to get you out of this, Sasha. There has to be another way." Besides, what would the ask be next time? Kidnap someone? "Break off the affair and we'll deal with the consequences together. I can help you through it."

"It's not that simple," Sasha countered, the desperation in her voice sent up more of those warning flares.

"Maybe it can be. You need to separate yourself from this man, Sasha. This sounds like a toxic relationship if he's asking you to spy on someone else. The best thing for you to do right now is to hang up the phone with me, call the guy, and tell him the affair is over. Explain that you can't see him anymore and he needs to go back to his wife and kids if he has them," she explained.

"He's married and he does have kids but that's not the problem." Again, the panic in her voice sent another shiver racing down Romy's spine.

"Whoever is blackmailing you will have nothing to work with if you end the affair." Romy hated playing the whole 'tough love' routine but what choice did she have? Sasha was going to have to learn at some point. Guilt niggled at Romy. She'd always felt responsible for her younger sister.

"Romy, stop. I'm pregnant."

Those last two words changed everything. They also sucked the air out of the room.

"I need your help, Romy. *My baby* needs her aunt. I wouldn't call you if I wasn't desperate. There's no one else I can contact. You're my best friend and my only family now that Dad is gone. Please. Help me. You know I wouldn't ask if there was another way. Please."

More of that guilt slammed into Romy. This time with the force of a hurricane. The same old tapes wound through her thoughts. How different would Sasha's life be if Romy had intervened sooner? The girls shared a father but grew up with different mothers under opposite circumstances. It wasn't until Romy's father broke down in front of her about her younger half-sister that Romy began to understand how bad the situation must be. Her father felt helpless. He had a criminal record and was behind on child support payments. Romy's mother had refused to fight for a child who wasn't hers despite Romy's desperate pleas.

When Romy turned nineteen and got her first apartment, she challenged Sasha's mother for custody and won. At twelve years old, Sasha had been withdrawn to the point of barely speaking. Romy had been the first to get through to her and even that was tentative the first few years. Their father helped with money and Romy worked her way through a two-year degree in a community college while making certain she would be home after school every day for Sasha. Times had been tough but they'd gotten through. Or so Romy had believed. When their father died in an unexpected car crash Sasha's senior year of high school, she'd packed up and gone on the road with a guy in a band.

Six months later, she'd shown up at Romy's door, broke, tired, and needing to sober up.

Romy had taken her sister in and given her a place to recuperate. Getting through to her, though, had always proved elusive. There'd been moments. Sparks. Times when Sasha would talk to Romy about a future. Sasha would take steps toward signing up to take her GED and she'd make progress with studying for it. Then, something would trigger a memory and Sasha would retreat. She would make a series of bad choices, which often included disappearing before showing up at Romy's door again weeks or sometimes months later, broke and desperate.

As long as Sasha was willing to try, Romy had sworn to herself she would do everything she could to help her sister. But this? This was too big of an ask.

"You have to involve the law, Sasha," Romy said. "This sounds serious."

This wasn't running away with a cute drummer only to find out months later she wasn't as special to him as she'd believed. That particular disaster had had a wife back home and Sasha had been nothing more to him than a good time on the road. She'd been broken, devastated.

Romy had gathered her sister up in her arms, welcomed her inside their small shared apartment, and then one-by-one helped her pick up the pieces before coming up with a new plan.

"Forget I said anything, Romy. I'll find a way to deal with it," Sasha said. She didn't hang up. Instead, she sat on the line, crying softly into the receiver.

"Fine. I'll help. But all I'm going to do is take the job and see if there's anything to find out in the first place," Romy relented. She always did. There wasn't much she wouldn't do to get her baby sister out of trouble, no matter how big her initial protest might be. Plus, Romy had sold her small business and had time on her hands.

"I'll call back with more details, Romy. Thank you. Thank you. Everything will be arranged, and I'll text you the address." Sasha sniffled a few times like she was trying to get her arms around her emotions.

"I get to see you in person once a week on Sundays," Romy stated. She didn't trust these people—whoever they were—any farther than she could throw them. "Tell them that. I mean it."

"I will," Sasha promised. "Romy..."

"Yes."

"I promise this is the last time I'm going to ask you to do something like this for me. The baby changes everything. I'm going to be the mom she deserves." Sasha had made other promises before, so Romy couldn't risk getting too caught up in the moment no matter how much she wanted to. She so desperately wanted Sasha to get on the right track, especially now that she was going to be a mother.

A mother? Romy could scarcely think of her sister in those terms. But before Romy could respond to her sister, Sasha hung up.

ERIC FIREBRAND WALKED into the kitchen of the main house where his brother Adam, Adam's wife Prudence, and their baby Angel had taken up residence. The main house had belonged to their grandfather and the once empty halls were now filled with laughter and occasionally the baby's tears.

One by one, several of his brothers had found the loves of their lives since summer started. Eric was beginning to believe there was something in the water. Something he needed to avoid like the plague.

"Coffee?" Adam asked.

"No, thanks," Eric responded. He didn't plan to drink the water around here, even if it had a dark roast blend in it. He held up his travel mug. "Brought my own."

Adam shot his brother a confused look, which caused Eric to smile. Four of his brothers fell down the same rabbit hole in a span of two months. He had no plans to follow suit, which meant avoiding the water. Just in case.

"Have you met the new office assistant yet?" Adam asked.

"That's what I came here for," Eric responded.

Everyone had been asked to stop by and introduce themselves to the new hire. The woman who must be Dawn Driver walked into the kitchen.

"Mind if I interrupt long enough to get a refill?" Dawn held up a coffee mug. She had to be five feet seven inches with legs that looked like she could play volleyball for a living. Hair that was black as night fell to her shoulders in long waves. Thick, black eyelashes framed powder blue eyes and a cream-colored minidress and boots with teal inlay highlighted those long legs of hers.

"Be my guest." Eric stepped aside as he tried to clear the frog in his throat. He shot a warning look at Adam, who wore the biggest smirk.

"My brother is a genius with the books," Adam said, patting Eric on the shoulder. "He'll be happy to answer any questions you have."

"Is she handling the books from now on?" Eric asked. His question netted a raised eyebrow from the black-haired beauty.

"It's what I was hired to do," she quickly countered

before lifting a shoulder. "But if you're not comfortable with it, we can discuss what my responsibilities should be while I'm here."

"I don't mind keeping the job. It'd take longer for me to explain it to you anyway." Eric wasn't real comfortable handing over any of the family financial information to a stranger. Firebrand Ranch business had always been handled by a Firebrand.

Based on Adam's expression, eyebrows knitted together and his mouth in a frown, he didn't approve of the tact Eric was taking.

"There's plenty other stuff to do in the office of a cattle ranch this time of year," Eric defended.

Dawn's gaze bounced from Eric to Adam and back. "I'm set up in your grandfather's office, in case anyone needs me. I should probably get back to it."

"How about we give you a different spot for the time being?" Eric began before receiving another look from his brother.

Adam turned to Dawn. "Will you excuse me and my brother for a few minutes?"

"Happy to help any way I can," she said, replacing the coffee pot as she finished her refill. "Where would you like me to wait in the meantime?"

"Go on back to my grandfather's office for now. I'll be in later to talk about where we'll set you up on a more permanent basis while you're here." Adam motioned toward the hallway from which she came.

"Nice meeting you," she said to Eric about the time he realized he never introduced himself. He blew out a sharp breath, realizing that he wasn't exactly leaving the best impression on their temporary hire. With his father in the hospital after a heart attack and their mother spending twenty-four-seven at his side, Eric was aware of the fact they needed the help. He didn't like it, but his parents played big roles in keeping the place running and their absence would soon take a toll on the business.

"Same," he said to her before she disappeared down the hall.

Adam wheeled around on Eric.

"What was that all about?" The spark in Adam's eyes said a whole lot about his frustration.

Eric held up his mug in defense. "I could have handled that better."

"You think?" Adam quipped.

"I don't know. The thought of having someone digging around our family business just doesn't sit right with me," Eric admitted.

"It's a little late for that now, don't you think?" Adam fired the question at Eric.

"Fair point," Eric stated. He was late to the game and should have thrown his two cents in before. But then the idea had been floated yesterday morning and before he could come up with a decent argument, the temp was here.

"Why didn't you speak up at the family meeting before we made the call and brought someone in?" Adam pressed.

"To be honest, I didn't know *how* I would feel until a stranger walked into our family kitchen just now," Eric countered. "It just seems like we should pull in one of the others to help rather than use people we don't know."

"We can't get along with our uncle and cousins on a good day," Adam pointed out.

"That's not true of all of them," Eric countered.

"Right now, we don't know who we can trust or who will feed information back to Uncle Keifer. Plus, I don't have to remind you what's been going on between Kellan and

Corbin." Those were good points. Their brother Corbin had married Kellan's ex-wife, which sounded a whole lot worse than it was. Corbin and Liv had been best friends since third grade, and everyone knew the two should have ended up together. It took them a hot minute to figure out what everyone else knew, but they got there eventually. And, yes, Kellan had been caught up in the fray. Though he never should have swooped in on Liv in the first place if anyone asked Eric. His cousin was the one out of line, even though Kellan didn't see it the same way. He was still swearing off women while nursing a broken heart, and blaming his cousin for his heartbreak.

And then, on top of that, Uncle Keifer had started an unfair fight when he tried to run Liv out of town and buy up her family property, as revenge for hurting his son. Her relative got involved with Uncle Keif and her life ended up being threatened.

Adam had a point about the two sides of the family being at odds at the moment. At this point, it was starting to look like they would never make amends.

Eric's thoughts drifted back to the woman down the hall. Maybe someone neutral toward both sides of the family was exactly who they needed right now. Could he learn to trust her?

2

Romy was Dawn Driver now.

Standing in the hallway to Marshall Firebrand's office, she didn't feel right going inside now that one of his grandsons had objected to her being there in the first place. Panic seized her as she tightened her grip on the coffee mug, wondering what the two men in the kitchen were talking about. *Her,* said a small voice in the back of her mind. *Breathe.*

"You can go on ahead inside. I'm Eric, by the way."

The man was tall, well over six feet—maybe six and a half—and muscled. The word *tank* came to mind when describing him, but it was more than that. He had a strong masculine presence that awakened parts of her that had no business being aroused at work. Eric Firebrand was the complete package; chiseled jawline, interesting combination of brown hair and green eyes, sex appeal in buckets. With arms like bands of steel, he looked like trouble in the best possible way. An attraction was out of the question no matter how much her body hummed with need while he stood so close to her.

"R-Dawn," she stammered, cursing herself for the almost slip. She was Dawn now. *Dawn. Dawn. Dawn.* Maybe if she repeated the name a few more times it would stick. Her life might very well depend on remembering, not to mention Sasha's. People as wealthy as the Firebrands wouldn't take lightly to someone spying on their business. Being here was the worst of bad ideas. Romy needed to find a way out of this before she slipped up and got herself caught. Jail would be the least of her problems if one of these guys figured out what she was up to.

More of that panic gripped her, causing her breathing to shallow and her body to tremble.

Eric looked her up and down, studying her. This must be it. The jig was up. He had to know she was a fraud and a liar. It was most likely written all over her face. For some odd reason the inscription in her middle school yearbook came to mind: Romy Nelson: Least likely to rob a bank. She didn't have the nerve for it or for any other crime, and this was most definitely illegal, no matter how much her sister had tried to convince Romy it was harmless.

"I apologize for the way I acted earlier," Eric said with more compassion in his voice than she deserved.

"It's fine," she quickly countered, trying her level best not to get distracted by those beautiful green eyes of his.

"No, it isn't. Not in this house." His words had a finite tone to them and he had a sense of calm she wished she could borrow, or at the very least lean into. "We don't...*I* don't think it's fine. You're here to help and you don't deserve to be on the receiving end of my frustration at the fact my father had a heart attack and there's nothing any of us can do to fix it."

"I'm really sorry." Well, now Romy felt even worse. She had been made aware there'd been a death in the family, a grandfather. But this? A family already in mourning, that had been dealt another blow? She shouldn't be here. "I'm probably in the way. I can..."

She started backing away from Eric, but he stopped her with a hand on her arm. All kinds of fire and electric sparks traveled up her arm with the contact.

The man locked onto her gaze and held it. "You're right where you belong as far as I'm concerned."

Those words were a knife to the center of her chest. Was there any way to back out of this nightmare? She could bolt now, and then what? Sasha would still be in trouble. The situation might even be worse for her now that Romy had agreed to do this terrible thing. She never should have compromised herself. Everything about this felt wrong and she didn't want to face the mirror until this was over with. She needed to finish the job and get out.

"Thank you," she finally offered.

He took his hand off her arm and she immediately felt its absence. Then, he held his hand out toward the office. "After you."

Romy walked inside and took the closest seat facing the large mahogany desk. It looked hand-carved and held a prominent spot in the room. Bookshelves lined two walls and there was a laptop on a foldout desk with a smaller chair pushed under on one of them. She would rather work there, off to the side, if she was being honest. The small space would keep her positioned with her side to the door so she could see who came and went. The desktop sat next to a window that looked over an impressive yard that would probably have a whole lot more green grass if the state wasn't in the middle of a two-year drought.

In a surprising move, Eric took the chair next to her and she had a moment of realization. From what she'd discovered online, his grandfather had been a bigger than life figure. Eric might be uncomfortable sitting in the man's chair.

"I handle a lot of the back-office accounting. I'm also responsible for ensuring the right tags get on the right calves and the paperwork matches up," he started. "Do you have a lot of experience working the office of a cattle ranch?"

She shook her head. "I'm a quick study and I have owned a business, which I sold successfully."

"Mind if I ask what made you want to work here?" He cocked an eyebrow.

"To be perfectly honest, I'm still figuring out my next move. This job is temporary and I'm bad at sitting at home twiddling my thumbs." She hoped the explanation would suffice. She'd been as honest as she could.

He studied her for few seconds before nodding his head.

"Understandable," he said. "I wouldn't be good at sitting around doing nothing, either."

"Then, how can I help?" she asked, grateful to think about something besides the fact she shouldn't be here.

"We're in the time of year where we perform our herd-health measures, cut hay, and perform pasture maintenance," Eric continued.

She had no idea what kind of paperwork that involved but she was good with a computer and knew several spreadsheet programs. At twenty, she'd started her own baking business that had been bought out by a local restaurant in Austin two months ago. The profit would keep her in her downtown apartment for several years but she needed to dig her hands into a new project. She'd be lost without a purpose.

"The majority of our calves have already sold through

auction and will leave mid-August, so we'll need to make certain their paperwork is in order," he continued.

The business side of cattle ranching sounded interesting.

"Do you sell any locally?" she asked.

"We help out a few restaurants throughout the year." He nodded. "But most are sold through auction. Other than that, we continue work in the hayfield well into the fall. Come November, we start our cycle over again with calving. And that's cattle ranching in a nutshell. The work is different with each season."

"Sounds like you're always busy," she remarked in a little bit of awe over the amount of hard work that must go into the process of running an operation the size of this one. Her small business had been a handful, and she'd loved every minute. It had consumed her, though. Plus, she'd had very little in the way of a life outside of work.

He rewarded her with a smile that sent warmth to all kinds of places.

"You could say that," he said. "But this is nothing like calving season."

"Do you ever take time off?" She probably shouldn't be asking personal questions, except that curiosity got the best of her.

This time, he chuckled and it was a low rumble that started deep in his chest. It was about the sexiest sound she'd ever heard and was pretty certain she blushed after hearing it. With him sitting this close, it was impossible to hide the heat rising up her neck and toward her cheeks.

Breathe.

"Ranchers rarely take a day off, let alone a whole week," he said. "It's a way of life more than anything else and takes a special breed of person to stick it out."

She picked up her coffee mug at the same moment he lifted his to his mouth. The saying, *Great minds think alike,* invaded her thoughts. Her first day at work was off to a better start now. The only way this could tank was if she actually slipped up and said her real name. The thought practically caused Romy's throat to close up. Her chest squeezed and she needed air. Maybe talking about herself a little would ease some of her anxious thoughts.

"I used to own a bakery until recently, and I closed shop every Monday but that didn't mean I got a day off," she admitted, realizing she'd just shared more than she probably should.

"A bakery? Must be why you didn't balk at the hours. A six a.m. start puts off a whole lot of people," Eric said.

Talking to him felt like the most natural thing when she should be keeping her guard up. This whole conversation was probably a bad idea. So, why did she want to keep talking when she needed to find the information and get out?

"Oddly enough, I'm not much of a morning person," the near-stranger admitted.

The admission surprised Eric.

"How is that so in your former line of work?" he asked.

"You do what you have to. You know?" Her eyes were the purest shade of blue and don't even get him started on her voice. She had the kind of musical quality that made him want to lean in closer. There was something vulnerable and yet very strong in the way she spoke. She had the kind of voice that he was certain made birds sing.

"That's the truth." Eric cleared his throat and then took a

sip of coffee. He'd been unfair to the temp hire and now he was overcompensating. He checked the time. Still no word from his mother today. It was early. He didn't want to wake her.

"What would you like me to get started on?" Dawn asked, glancing around the room. Her gaze landed on the laptop next to the window.

"How do you feel about doing a little inventory?" he asked.

"Calves can't be much different than counting bags of flour," she quipped.

"I'll set you up over here." He motioned toward the laptop and could have sworn a smile crossed her lips—lips he had no business staring at or noticing how full and pink they were.

This was a sure sign Eric needed to get out of the house more. He was ogling the temp hire and couldn't remember the last decent date he'd had. Rather than chew on the thought, he moved to set her up at her spot. Eric had been working there in the last few days, unable and unwilling to take over the Marshall's desk.

Since the files were kept on the cloud, he didn't have to worry about which computer he used. They all pulled from the same place. He showed her how to match the inventory tags with the file in a matter of minutes. She was a quick study. Maybe bringing her here wasn't such a bad idea after all. She seemed to be working out well and he considered himself a good judge of character. She'd calmed down considerably after taking a few minutes to talk to her. It had been time well spent.

"I'll be in and out if you need anything," he said.

"Mind if I get your number?" She picked up her cell

phone. "I'd rather not sit idle if you need to be somewhere else on the property and I have a question."

Her work ethic was admirable. But then, she'd said she used to own a business. She would have had to have hustled to make it work.

He held out his hand and a look of panic crossed her features. What was that all about?

"I figured it was easier for me to program in the number myself, but it's no prob—"

"Right. No. It makes perfect sense." She handed over her cell but her initial reaction registered with him as unusual. He took note and moved on.

After programming in his number, he held out her phone. Their fingers grazed and electricity shot up his arm. *Whoa.*

Dawn was smart. She was beautiful. There was a distant quality about her that he couldn't quite pinpoint and yet it drew him in, made him want to learn more about her. There was something behind her eyes, a mystery that made him want to be cautious around her. It also caused a half dozen questions to pop into his mind but he figured asking them would scare her off.

Eric glanced at her ring finger on her left hand. Relief he had no right to own washed over him when there was no gold band and no tan line. Since he wasn't winning the war against his curiosity, he decided to take a breather.

"I'll be back in a while," he said, taking a step back, quashing questions like who she was and where she came from. He wanted to know more about the mystery woman. This also seemed like a good time to remind himself that just because she wasn't wearing a ring didn't mean she was single.

"Okay," she said and her voice dropped to practically a

whisper.

Before Eric asked something that crossed the line of professionalism, he exited the room. Those piercing eyes would stick in his thoughts far longer than he wanted to allow. The questions crept in despite his best efforts to quash them. Who was she? What did she do when she wasn't starting and running a bakery? Why had she shut down when he'd asked about her business? And then, what about the incident with her phone? She seemed protective. He chalked it up to being in a new environment and maybe out of her comfort zone working a ranch.

Digging around in her employment file would draw unwanted attention to him. Eric had already poured it on a little too strong with Adam a little while ago. Convincing his brother that Eric didn't mind having a temp after getting worked up about it would take some doing if Adam caught Eric nosing around in her employment file.

And what did he expect to find there? She had been offered a living arrangement here on the ranch while she was employed. It was easier that way. She would get Sundays off but didn't mind working six days a week.

When Eric really thought about it, she was either saving money for something or enjoying a break from running a business. Cattle ranching was in his blood and he couldn't imagine doing anything else, but the commitment was more than a full-time job. He didn't know the first thing about running a bakery, but she would be used to being her own boss.

More questions about the new hire crept in. First day jitters would be normal for anyone. Hers bordered on paranoid. If he spent more time around her, maybe he could get answers. Yes. That would do it. He'd have to spend more time around her. For answers.

3

E ric gave Dawn some time to get settled and into a routine before returning to the Marshall's office before lunch. The second he stepped inside, she gasped. There was most definitely something going on here.

"Didn't mean to startle you," he said. Asking outright would probably send her into a deeper panic and he doubted she'd tell him what was really going on. His mind snapped to all kinds of possibilities, none he liked. The first was whether or not an abusive relationship was involved. He hated the fact this was the place his mind went to. The truth that a woman's biggest threat was someone she knew and trusted caused him to grind his back teeth.

"It's fine," she said. She'd used the same term earlier when she was trying to smooth everything over. Just like last time, there was no real enthusiasm in the word.

"I thought we could take a walk around the property for lunch, introduce you to anyone who might be around." If he was going to be working closely with her for a few weeks, and that was his hope because it meant his father's condition was improving, Eric figured he better get to know her.

"Okay-y-y-y. Sure." She sounded uncertain and, for a second, his ego took a hit. "I brought food, so there's no need to worry about feeding me."

"You're welcome to make yourself at home on the ranch." Eric needed to show her the fridge. There was enough food inside to feed a small army. Of course, with nine sons on his side of the family alone, plus all the ranch hands, an army's worth of groceries was in order.

Of course, a few of his brothers had decided to bolt after high school, vowing never to return. His brother Dane had made his way back home and it was Eric's hope the others would too. Call it selfish, but he wanted his family to take their rightful place as heirs. Plus, blood ran thick in a Firebrand and he loved each of his brothers. He couldn't say the same for some of his cousins, and he'd never been close to his uncle. But then again, Eric wasn't exactly close to his father either, and recent revelations about the man had Eric's respect levels dropping about as low as they could go.

Dawn closed up the laptop and tucked her purse underneath the desk in the far corner. Before getting up, she reached down like she was making sure it was secure.

"Have you seen your room yet?" he asked, figuring he could give her the whole tour while he was at it.

"Not yet. I think my suitcases are still parked at the front door," she admitted.

"We can start there." He walked down the hall to where her things sat like gargoyles guarding the entrance. "Just these two?"

"Yes. I can help with..."

He picked both up before she could finish her sentence.

"Those are heavy. Are you sure you don't want help?" she asked.

"I got it." He almost laughed. If she thought these were

heavy, she had no idea the kind of strength working a cattle business required. He walked her to the staircase to the east wing from a separate hallway off the kitchen and to the room Raleigh had used while she stayed here with her band. Raleigh was a local who'd become a huge success in the country music scene and had recently married into the family. His brother Brax was on tour with his wife, holding off on a proper honeymoon until she met her commitments to her fans. Eric had yet to see someone so devoted to their supporters.

"This whole place is for me?" The temp stopped at the door rather than walk inside.

"It is. Where would you like to set these?" he asked.

"Anywhere is fine." The awe in her voice caused his chest to swell with pride. While the Marshall had lived here, the place had seemed empty. Now, it teemed with family coming and going, and his brother Adam lived here in the west wing with his wife and daughter. A house this big should be filled with kids and grandkids as far as Eric was concerned. Otherwise, it was just a huge museum. "You do know that I have an apartment downtown in Austin."

"You're going to be here six days a week. You should be comfortable." Eric set the bags next to the closet door. As he turned around, she took a few steps inside but stayed close to the door. Did she feel like she needed a quick exit? Maybe he could put her at ease by telling her a little bit about the family.

"Have you heard of Raleigh Perry?" he asked.

"Who hasn't? She's huge and that new single she put out, *The Loft,* is probably her best work." The admiration and respect in Dawn's voice struck a chord with Eric.

"This was her room while she stayed here recently," he

said. "And the loft she wrote about is in that barn right there." He walked to the window and pointed.

The woman joined him, standing beside him where he could breathe in her scent, a mix of exotic flowers and clean perfume.

He cleared his throat.

"Why are there two identical barns?" she asked.

"My grandfather liked to pit his only two sons against each other. Said it made them stronger to compete. He had two barns built and two houses for each of them," he admitted.

"Oh," she said and there was a whole lot going on in that one word. Was she too polite to state the obvious? It was a messed-up way to view family.

"What about their mother? She put up with it?" she asked.

"I'm not sure she felt like she had a choice. Our grand-mother passed away when we were young, so I barely remember her. She was kind and loved to cook. She sang all the time and the few memories I have of her are all good. But you know what they say about memories," he said. "Turns out, they're just pieced together fragments we collect along the way as kids."

"I read that somewhere too," she said. "Kind of fasci-nating what the human brain can and can't do, isn't it?"

He nodded.

"It's wild how little we actually know about how our minds work," she continued, her face lighting up.

He'd clearly touched on a topic of interest to her.

"I'm sure we're capable of a whole lot more than we real-ize," he agreed, capitalizing on the common ground.

"Exactly," she said. "Plus, you know, there have to be ways of healing people who have been damaged emotionally that we haven't even tapped into yet. Especially those with PTSD or who have been traumatized in some way."

Eric took note of the emphasis she'd placed on helping others. The way she spoke about it with distance made him think she referred to someone else and not herself. Was there someone in her life who'd been hurt? Who she was trying to help?

At least his go-to fear of a boyfriend being the culprit seemed like the wrong track. Good. The thought of any person hurting someone they were supposed to care about caused his hands to fist.

This beauty was opening up and he hoped to get answers to a few more questions before this conversation was over.

~

THIS CONVERSATION NEEDED to be over. Romy felt herself getting more and more comfortable with her employer and she needed to cut it out before she slipped again. "Can we go see the barn?"

"Yeah. Sure," Eric said. The change in direction seemed to give him momentary whiplash but it was necessary to her survival.

Spying on a stranger was one thing. Learning about his family and getting to know him made this feel personal. Could she shut down her emotions and hurt someone she genuinely liked? To be fair, she didn't want to like Eric. Or any of the other Firebrands for that matter. Why did he have to be so down-to-earth and easy to talk to? He was attractive to the point of a distraction. One she couldn't afford.

His easy-going nature made being with him feel as natural as breathing in air. Those were more thoughts she needed to erase. How nice would he be toward her if he knew the real reason she was there? An icy chill raced down her spine at the thought. Because the guy was also strong enough to crack a two-by-four in half with his bare hands. And yet, he didn't seem to have a violent streak in him.

Romy had dated one of those charming-on-the-surface guys when she was too young to know better. Andrew had been attractive. He came from money and he knew all the right things to say to get her to go on a date with him. In the beginning, it had been easy to make excuses for some of his behavior, like when he got snippy with a hostess because their table was taking too long to get ready. Or his behavior in traffic when someone cut him off. His anger had gotten them in more than one scary situation at red lights. Austin traffic was a force unto itself, and yet he'd displayed road rage consistent with someone who had anger issues.

When she broke off the relationship, Andrew had doubled down. Showing up unannounced and unwanted at her favorite coffee shop, and then making a scene when she got up to leave. Stalking her favorite taco stand at lunchtime, and then crowding her when she needed physical space.

The guy finally got the hint when he moved onto someone else, but she'd had to stand her ground with him to get him to backoff after threatening to get a restraining order. Part of her wanted to place a warning label on his social media: *Beware! Not who you think he is.*

Moving on and never looking back had always been her talent. Andrew might have been an extreme case, but she'd kept her running shoes next to the door on every relationship since. Sasha used to tease her sister for being hard on men she dated. The truth was that Romy didn't have time to invest in a real relationship. Plus, how many guys would understand Romy's need to help Sasha? Or start a business from the ground up? Or be alone when life caved in around her?

Following Eric down the stairs, she tried not to stare at his impressive back. *Or backside*, she thought wryly.

"You'll find everything you could want or need in here." Eric crossed the incredible kitchen that would be every chef's dream, and made a beeline for the fridge. He opened the French doors.

"The fridge in my bakery would be jealous of this one," she quipped. Had it been a mistake to share that piece of information about her? All it would take was one search to discover Dawn Driver had never owned a bakery in Austin. A knot formed in her chest thinking about the possibility of getting caught.

It wasn't just *her* life on the line. Sasha had no options. *Sasha.* The pregnancy announcement had been a game-changer. Romy was still trying to wrap her mind around Sasha becoming a mother. The fact her sister was in trouble again sat hard on Romy's chest. What had Sasha gotten Romy into now?

Eric's face broke into a wide smile in a show of perfectly straight, white teeth. Hot didn't begin to describe the man when he smiled. Her heart melted like butter on the side-walk in the August heat. Her knees went weak, threatening to buckle, and she finally understood how that could happen. She'd dismissed the saying as silly before Eric Firebrand.

But then a sexy cowboy with a smile like his should come with a very different warning label: *Danger! Heart at risk.*

"It's always stocked and you're welcome to take anything you want from here. It's communal and you won't hurt anyone's feelings by heating up a pre-cooked meal. It's what they're here for." Eric closed the door. "Feel free to cook if you'd rather."

"Oh no. I'd rather not," she stated with a little more conviction than intended.

His eyebrow shot up in surprise. "I'm not one of those jerks who believe women belong in the kitchen, so don't take this the wrong way."

"Didn't think you were," she said without hesitation. Again, the man's smile would cause water to boil on a cold stove.

"I just figured since you owned a bakery that you would like the kitchen," he clarified.

"Makes sense." She shrugged.

"But, what?" He didn't seem ready to let her off the hook without an explanation.

"Baking is totally different than cooking," she pointed out.

"True." He nodded.

"I love sweets. That's why I started the business in the first place. Plus, I could work early in the morning and watch..." She cast her eyes down to the flooring. "Have the rest of the day to do whatever I wanted. The bakery closed at two o'clock."

"Where was it located?" He seemed genuinely interested, which made it all the more difficult to stop talking.

But she had to.

"Austin." She walked toward the backdoor, stopping as she opened it. "Are you coming?"

He jogged up to her, so she exited. Quickly. Because the last thing she needed was to breathe in his spicy male scent. *Sasha is in trouble*, Romy reminded. She was here solely for her sister.

Part of her wondered if Sasha would be so quick to

damage the family once she met them. It was so much easier to hurt strangers. So far, Romy had met Adam and Eric, both decent people. Good people. This whole ordeal would go a lot smoother if they were jerks.

Or would it?

Stealing from a bad person didn't absolve her for being the one to commit the act. Didn't it make her a bad person too? It did, however, feel like an even bigger crime to steal information from a nice family. Worse yet, a family that was in mourning and who'd almost lost their father.

Romy exhaled, thinking about the old gothic-style church in downtown Austin with all the stairs. There wasn't enough holy water in the place to fix spying on good people like the Firebrands.

Again, she wished there was another way to help Sasha. One that didn't involve a felony, which this had to be. The only way to get through this was to hold her cards closer to her chest, keep her head down, and finish what she came here to do. No more talking about the bakery, or anything about her past. No more opening up to Eric Firebrand. No more wishing she could stare into those green eyes and spill all her secrets. Especially no more of the last one.

"Ready?" Eric palmed a key he'd retrieved from his pocket.

"I thought we were going to the barn." She stopped, not bothering to hide her surprise.

"Change of plans," he said, heading in the direction of a parked truck.

"Do I get to know where we're headed?" Panic that he'd figured her out was a stalker in a dark alley. Had she been 'made?' Was this it? Was he planning to drive her some-where off property and drop her on the side of the road?

Romy would deserve it for agreeing to spy on his family.

Her anxiety shot through the roof. It didn't help that she still hadn't heard from Sasha after texting first thing this morning. Her cell was in quiet-mode and she desperately wanted to check it. *Breathe.*

She wanted nothing more than to get back to work, find out whatever would save her sister, and get far away from Firebrand Ranch.

"I'm taking you to the hospital," Eric said. "Thought you might like to meet the people you're helping."

Romy sucked in a breath before she could stop herself. Eric turned. She forced a smile, and hoped like everything he bought the move.

4

D awn's reaction caught Eric off guard. What had her so scared?

He had half a mind to force the issue, asking her outright what was going on. That seemed about as productive as planting weeds and calling it a crop. Given enough time, he'd find out what was bothering her. Since he'd be spending the workday close to her side, it was only a matter of time before she became comfortable enough with him to talk. He already noted she liked figuring out the inner workings of the mind. His guess that someone who had traumatized her resurfaced, or, possibly, she was trying to help someone who had been abused.

The drive to the hospital was quiet. Dawn clasped her hands so tightly on her lap there couldn't possibly be any blood flow. She sank a little lower in her seat like she was nervous about being seen. Or was Eric building evidence of a theory he'd already developed?

He parked at Lone Star Pass General, exited the driver's seat, and then moved to the passenger side. Eric knew full well the woman was capable of opening her own door, doing so for her was like breathing air. The move was ingrained in him, and he liked the show of respect.

Dawn climbed out, taking the hand he offered. Again, a burning heat sizzled from the point of contact shooting warmth spreading through him. Once she let go, he rubbed his thumb and fingers together, the feel of her imprinted on him.

The sun was high in the sky. The forecast said triple-digits were in order. It didn't help that the state was in a two-year drought and the concrete in August already seemed hot enough to melt the soles of his boots. No rain in sight and there wasn't a cloud in the sky. If it kept on like this, they'd have to move the cattle. They were already bringing in hay like there was no tomorrow. Water rights could cause wars among rival ranchers. The Firebrands owned more than their fair share. The livestock was good there. But rain would solve a few problems.

Dawn was reserved, not shy. It was an important distinction that Eric had noted over the years. She was quiet all the way inside the hospital, on the elevator, and in the hallway leading to his father's room. She seemed to be deep in thought, taking it all in. Her lips thinned and lines scored her forehead. Her face muscles appeared taut. All signs of distress. Then, she abruptly stopped in the hallway before entering his father's room. Panic vibrated off her in palpable waves as she stood at the threshold.

"This seems like a place for family," she said, shaking her head. "I'm not comfortable going inside."

"Okay," he said for lack of a better response. He couldn't force her to walk in the room and being at a hospital seemed to be a trigger for something bad in her background. His intention hadn't been to make her uncomfortable. Given how quiet she'd been on the way over, she was having a serious internal response to coming here. "If you want to take a seat out here somewhere, I'll just be a minute."

"There's probably a vending machine somewhere on this floor." She glanced around and the panicked look returned. "I'll find it and get something to drink."

He didn't think this was the time to point out she hadn't brought her purse with her. Her wide eyes told him to let her walk away and get some much-needed air.

"Sounds like a plan." He pulled out his wallet. "Mind getting a Coke for me?"

"Not at all." Relief washed over her that she would have a legitimate errand.

"Then, you'll have to allow me to buy yours as well," he continued, peeling off several ones.

For a half second, she looked prepared to debate his offer. She must have realized she didn't have any money with her when she let out the breath she'd been holding and took his offering. "Only if you'll take it out of my pay."

"We'll work out a deal," he said, figuring she wouldn't take no for an answer.

"Fine," she said. There was that word again.

Looking relieved she didn't have to go inside a patient room, she turned and bounded down the hallway in the opposite direction. Eric waited a few seconds. His curiosity was growing when it came to the former bakery owner. Despite her fear and the big question mark surrounding her, there was a pull to her like nothing he'd ever experienced. Attraction? Yes. No arguing there. But it was so much more. His protective instincts flared even though it was obvious she could take care of herself. She was sharp and strong, yet at the same time managed to pull off a surprisingly vulnerable side.

Rather than stand there and recount all her good quali-

ties, Eric tapped a couple of times on the door before stepping inside. The room was a double. There was a wall of
windows with southern exposure, letting in all the sunlight.
Good. His father had always been an outdoor person. Being
cooped up inside with no light would be worse than a death
sentence to a rancher.

"Eric." His mother's face broke into a wide smile as she
waved him over. She sat in a lounger with a blanket over her
legs, pencil in hand working out a crossword puzzle.

His father's heavy breathing said he was asleep. Eric
didn't want to disturb the man, so he practically tiptoed
across the room. He took a seat on the windowsill next to his
mother after a brief hug, leaning his back against the
tempered glass. Lucia Firebrand reached over and took his
hand in hers, squeezing before kissing his knuckles. Eyes
bright, her face lit up with his visit. Guilt stabbed him for
not stopping by sooner. It had only been a couple of days
since the heart attack and he'd been busy at the ranch ever
since. Still, seeing his mother's excitement over him being
here was a good reminder to come back soon. If he was
being honest, he' hoped his father would be released and
home before Eric had to make the drive again. Everyone
would feel better if they knew he was out of the woods.

"How's Dad doing?" Even from here, Eric could see his
father's ashen skin. Brodie Firebrand had never looked old
to Eric until now, until seeing him lying on his back with his
mouth slightly open, asleep.

"Doctor says it's good news. He needs a few more days of
rest and observation before he'll be released," his mother
whispered.

"Sounds promising," he said, mustering up as much
encouragement in his voice as he could.

She smiled.

Eric might not be close to his father but his mother was another story. Despite the recent discovery that his brother Brax wasn't her biological child, and the upset the news had caused in the family, his mother had always been the kindest, most honest person he knew.

Her smile faded when she said, "It took a lot out of him."

She seemed to have the hardest time calling the medical condition a heart attack. The two had been in a fight when the episode had happened, and Eric wondered if his mother felt responsible in some way. She'd moved into the main house for a few days and his father had been emotionally wrecked. Not that Brodie Firebrand didn't deserve it. He'd had multiple affairs early on in their marriage and had convinced her to lie to Brax. Walking in on one of those affairs as a child and being forced to cover was the reason his brother Dane had signed up for the military and moved as far away from the family ranch as possible. But none of this was her fault.

Eric gently squeezed her hand—a hand that was bonier than he remembered. It was a strange feeling watching his parents age, seeing them morph from vibrant people to a shadow of their former selves.

Brodie Firebrand had always seemed invincible to Eric. A combination of age and stress had caught up to his father. Lies. Eric couldn't stand them. Finding a way to maintain respect for his father after all the lies started coming to light would prove a challenge. For now, Eric planned to focus on helping his mother get through this. Based on the look on her face, she was holding on by a thread.

"How's Angel?" she asked. Of course she would ask about her only granddaughter. After having nine sons— sons she loved—she'd made no secret about wishing for a girl.

"As perfect as ever." Eric was barely an uncle, so he couldn't imagine becoming a father. A couple of his brothers were now fathers. Parenthood looked good on them. Eric wasn't sure he ever wanted kiddos, especially as messed up as the Firebrands were. Uncle Keif and Eric's father had made fighting with each other a full-time sport. To the point Eric and his brothers wondered if his father even knew they existed.

"And little Lucas?" His mother referred to the five-month-old son Dane was in the process of adopting.

"Terrible," Eric teased.

His mother swatted at him playfully. Her face broke into another wide smile behind weary eyes. "You're kidding me."

"How are you?" he asked in as sincere a tone as he could muster.

"Me?" She swatted air. "I'm good."

"No. Really. How are *you*?" Eric had no plans to let her get away with pretending her world hadn't recently collapsed.

"Brax called a little while ago." She brought her hand to cover her heart and Eric wondered if she realized she'd done it.

"How is it being on the road with Raleigh and the band?" Eric leaned his head against the glass. He couldn't imagine leaving the ranch for weeks at a time. He'd miss the work, the daily grind. Brax loved working the ranch, so Eric wasn't sure how his brother was coping.

"Good, he says." Her smile was genuine. She had babysat Raleigh in her youth. Mom had followed Raleigh's career and had even inspired a song, according to the country singer. Raleigh had been a good kid who'd grown into a woman Brax had fallen head over heels for. "Being with his wife makes it all worthwhile."

"I guess," Eric said.

"People are saying there's something in the water at the ranch." Mom winked, and he knew that look. She wasn't getting away with it.

"Precisely why I'm not drinking it," Eric shot back. He wasn't having any of this discussion.

"Love is a funny thing." She wagged her finger in the air. "Mark my words that when it finds you, you have no power to stop it."

"Sounds awful." He made a face like he'd bit into a sour grape.

Mom laughed and it filled the room with a soft sigh.

"Maybe someday you'll find a person who makes your heart feel like it's going to break free from your chest every time she is near."

He hated to tell his mother the news. The woman in the hallway came dangerously close, but he had no intention of falling in love with her or anyone else for that matter.

"I better head back," he said, not wanting to leave the temp in the hallway forever.

A soft knock at the door caused his pulse to race.

"Come in."

Romy moved toward the sound of Eric's voice, fighting the images that were assaulting her. Images of her baby sister in a room on a different floor, arm broken, face swollen, spirit shattered. On the children's ward, there were a lot more bright colors. There were balloons and stuffed animals meant to cheer kids up, and make them forget the horrors that brought them here in the first place. There was no such magic for a teenager sent to rescue the little sister she loved.

Romy took a few more tentative steps inside the room. It had been so very long since she'd been inside a hospital. She hoped to never need one. Although, that probably wasn't very realistic. At some point, she might like to have a child of her own. It would have to be with a very special man. Those seemed in short supply until she met Eric Firebrand.

All the reason even more guilt assaulted her at what she had to do.

"This is my mother, Lucia Firebrand." Eric stood up as Romy entered the room. *One step at a time*, she reminded.

"It's a pleasure to meet you." Romy tightened her grip on the Coke cans in her hands.

Eric walked over to her, his gaze taking her in. He seemed to sense something was wrong. She'd picked up on it earlier. As much as she wanted...*needed*...to unload everything going on in her mind since pulling up to the hospital, she reminded herself to keep her personal life private.

He took both drinks out of her hands and then set them on a tray. Linking their fingers, he walked her over to get a closer look at his mother.

Lucia Firebrand was a beautiful woman, despite the years marking her face. Her bright eyes and warmth was like stepping closer to the sun on a cold day.

"Nice to meet you, Mrs. Firebrand," she said. "I'm just sorry it isn't under better circumstances."

"This is life." The older woman shrugged. She looked to be of Italian descent. "Ups and downs."

Romy could relate to that sentence. Though, hers had had more downs than ups. That wasn't actually true, she corrected. She'd started a small business that was successful enough to attract an investor, who bought her out for a nice sum. She was lying low, looking for inspiration for her next move. There was a lot to be proud of in her life. So, why did she feel like a huge failure?

One word. *Family.*

What was it about family that could reduce a person to the quick? Not being able to save the one person Romy cared about more than anyone else on this earth cut deep.

"I hope your husband gets better soon," Romy said for lack of anything else to say. It was true, though. No one should have to be in a hospital for long.

"He will," she reassured.

Was Mrs. Firebrand comforting Romy? What a sweet woman.

"I was just telling my mom that you and I should head back to the ranch soon," Eric said.

"Thank you for the job," Romy said, thinking that meeting this woman was going to make her mission a whole lot harder to carry out. How could she go back and spy on a family she was beginning to care about?

"You're welcome," his mom said, batting her hand like it was nothing. "We can use the help and it's nice to have another woman in the house. We are growing our numbers." She smiled the warmest smile at her son before firing off a wink Romy decided not to ask about later.

"Mom's been on her own, surrounded by nothing but testosterone, for far too long according to her," Eric said with a chuckle. That low rumble in his chest sent vibrations rocketing through Romy. How was a man's laugh so sexy that it weakened her at the knees every single time she heard it? The need for warning labels were racking up. What was she up to now? Three? Four?

"I love my boys, don't get me wrong. But I'm ready to

have more women around," his mom admitted. Her cheeks flushed and her eyes sparkled. "Sue me."

"We better get going," Eric finally said.

Despite the warmth in his mother's smile, and the fact his presence calmed her nerves a level below panic, Romy could hardly wait to get out of there. She needed to have a conversation with her sister and tell her there was no way this plan was going to work. They needed to put their heads together and come up with a different solution. Maybe Sasha could go into hiding for a little while until this all blew over. Romy had enough cash stashed away to hold them for a while. They could go to someplace like Michigan, where no one would expect them to be.

"Thank you for stopping by," Mrs. Firebrand said before bringing her son into a hug. The exchange brought a surprising tear to Romy's eye at witnessing the tender moment happening.

"It really is lovely to meet you," Romy said before exiting the room. She checked her phone while they waited for an elevator. Still no response from Sasha.

"Everything all right?" Eric stood, arms folded across a massive chest, studying her.

"It's a family thing," she said.

He nodded.

Where was Sasha? And why wasn't she answering Romy's texts?

5

"Do you have siblings?" Eric asked once he and Dawn were back in the truck and on the road.

"One. A sister," she said quietly. "We have the same dad, different mothers."

"Is she older or younger than you?" he continued, wanting to get to know Dawn better. Her reaction to going into the hospital room sent up a few warning flares. He found himself in the position of wanting to help but not having the first idea how to go about it. Keeping her talking was the best way for him to find out.

"Younger," she supplied.

"Does she have to do with the 'family' issue you're having?" It was a bold question, but Eric genuinely wanted to know and he could only hope it came across the right way.

"Yeah." She blew out a sharp breath.

"Anything you want to talk about?" he figured he could capitalize on the moment.

"Not my story to tell." She shut the trail down pretty quick.

Rather than try to talk her into continuing down that thread, he changed the topic. In his experience, pushing for someone to open up usually had the opposite effect. He'd learned the lesson the hard way throughout various relationships. The idea especially hit home on his last one. He and Lynn Gable had had an on-again, off-again relationship for the last five years. Currently, they were off. This time, it needed to stick. Eric wouldn't normally put up with someone who couldn't make up their mind about being in a relationship with him, but Lynn had experienced an abusive boyfriend. She'd been gun shy and he'd been naïve enough to believe that, given enough space, she would come around.

Against his better judgment, he let her come back after she broke it off with him the first time. The second time, it had taken more convincing on her part. Then, somehow, it developed into a pattern.

It had been three months since he'd heard from Lynn. Enough time for him to get his head on straight and accept the fact the two of them weren't meant to be, no matter how much he enjoyed her company. Eric could never be with someone long-term who shut him out or could so easily walk away without warning.

Lynn had started seeing a counselor but could never bring herself to open up to him about what had really happened. As much as he cared about her, their relationship was like trying to grow corn in a dark box in dry soil.

Their last conversation had her asking him for time to work on herself. He'd stepped aside, wishing her the best of luck.

The woman seated next to him was another story. This was a work relationship and, he hoped, a friendship considering they'd be working together for the foreseeable future. In fact, if she worked out, he'd already thought about pitching the idea to offer her a permanent position. Of course, this might be a temporary stop until she figured out her next move. Now that he was getting more comfortable with her it seemed a shame to train someone just to let them go in a few weeks. Plus, the new hire could ease some of the burden of running the place from his parents.

"Can I ask why you hired me?" Dawn asked. "I get the impression you didn't want the help from the conversation with your brother earlier."

"True," he admitted, realizing how perceptive she was. Of course, he hadn't exactly been shy about his protest this morning in the kitchen. "I'll level with you."

She perked up, straightening her back.

"The thought of my parents needing help with the ranch they'd worked longer than I've been alive didn't sit right. I might not be close with my father, but he's always been a strong figure in my mind. Seeing him in a hospital bed feels all kinds of wrong," he admitted.

She was already nodding before he even finished.

"It's hard to see family at their weakest point," she said with a whole lot of compassion in her voice.

"Especially someone who has always been stronger than you," he added.

From the corner of his eye, he caught her giving him a once over.

"Somehow I doubt anyone is stronger than you," she said so low he almost missed it.

The comment made him chuckle.

"But I think I understand what you mean," she said and he could almost feel her cheeks heating. "It's difficult to see someone you've looked up to all your life crumble, or be at their weakest point."

"My mom blames herself for the heart attack," he said. "I can see it in her eyes."

"Why is that?"

"She'd been staying at the main house. He'd pressured her to keep silent about the fact one of my brothers was born out of an affair. Mom brought him up like one of her own and I have no doubt she couldn't love him more if he'd been her blood," he said.

"Sounds complicated," she said with another sigh.

"Aren't families always complex?"

"You can say that again." She pinched the bridge of her nose like she was staving off a headache.

The mention of family and her sister seemed to strike a chord for her.

In the rearview, Eric saw a blacked-out SUV barreling toward them on the two-lane road. What was up with this jerk? Eric figured the best move was to let the guy pass. "Hold tight, okay?"

"Why? What's going on?" She spun her head around and then sank into the seat like she was trying to make herself as small as possible.

This fell into the category of *abnormal reaction*.

Meanwhile, the angry driver nearly tapped Eric's bumper. Was road rage a trigger for her? He took a mental note and kept a steady hand on the wheel, keeping one eye on the SUV.

A quick glance at the passenger seat revealed Dawn's eyes were squeezed shut. Every muscle in her body tensed as she seemed to prepare for impact.

In the calmest voice he could muster, he said, "We're okay."

"Is it still back there?" Her face had gone bleached sheet white.

"Yes." He watched as the SUV came speeding up a couple more threatening times, stopping within inches of his vehicle before retreating. There was no license plate and the front windshield reflected the sun too much to get a good look at the driver.

Eric had a mind to stop his truck in the middle of the road, blocking both sides, so he could step out and see what this guy's real problem was. Before he could get too far down that path, the SUV made a sharp right.

"He's gone now," Eric said, keeping an eye on the rearview mirror just in case.

Dawn sat up and immediately checked the side view mirror. She exhaled when the road was clear, making him wonder if she'd been in some sort of accident. She was a puzzle. One he intended to find all the pieces to and fit them together if he was going to get comfortable enough to open the family books to her. Besides, after Lynn, he was done with secrets.

Maybe he could get answers if he probed a little more.

"I DOUBT he's coming back. Just a hothead."

Romy had serious doubts Eric's statement could be true. For one, why would a random SUV pick this moment to intimidate him? Or had the SUV been following them this whole time without them knowing it?

Icy fingers gripped her spine at the thought of being watched. She also wondered if the blacked-out SUV had anything to do with the fact her sister wasn't responding to texts?

The voice of reason spoke up, reminding her that Sasha often times went days or weeks, sometimes months, without returning messages. *This time is different*, her mind reasoned. It *had* to be different. Romy wasn't normally putting her life on the line to spy on someone else's family or buy her sister time. And what Sasha meant by that comment exactly? Buy time to do what? Figure out a different plan? One that didn't involve invading innocent people's privacy?

Romy took in a few slow, deep breaths. Getting worked up and letting her stress take over would only make everything worse. The *what ifs* were creeping in, and those were never good when it came to thinking about her sister.

Another *what if* stole the show. What if Romy told Eric what was really going on?

Shutting the idea down quickly, she tried to relax her shoulders. Her head was starting to throb, a sure sign she was overthinking the situation. At this point, she craved a hot bath, a cup of calming tea, and the rest of the afternoon off and. Something with lavender in the bath sounded like a small slice of heaven to her right then.

But, right now, she owed Eric an explanation for her actions a minute ago.

"I'm not a huge fan of wild drivers," she said by way of excuse. "When I was a kid, my dad used to get frustrated on the roads. He'd yell and flip people off any time they got too close or he believed they were driving distracted. Once, a guy pulled out a gun and shot through our windshield. The whole experience left a mark, and now I get stressed when another driver acts up."

"I'm sorry that happened to you. The way I see it, there's no reason to get worked up about something outside of your control." Eric's voice was a study in calm. *He* was a study in calm. The man's steady temperament kept her nerves a notch below panic and soothed her soul in places she'd long neglected.

And then reality dawned. What if the driver of the SUV circled back to the hospital? What if the two of them had just led the guy to Eric's parents? Panic tightened her chest, making it hard to breathe.

Romy reminded herself to calm down as her pulse shot through the roof. She needed to think this through properly and not react based on heightened emotion.

If the person forcing her to steal information from the family wanted to kill any one of them, wouldn't that have already happened? They certainly didn't need her around for the job. Plus, wouldn't that draw unwanted attention? Cause the Firebrands to increase security? Look over their shoulders everywhere they walked?

This line of thinking was rational. This made more sense. This was plausible.

Why would the SUV pick now to intimidate them? The only answer that made any sense was her. The driver was sending a message *to her*. She needed to stay focused and on task. The uneasy part was that she didn't even know who she was supposed to get this information to other than her sister. Who was ultimately behind this?

Romy realized she should have forced her sister to give the name of the father of her child to her, so she could begin to put together associations. As it was, she was flying blind.

Of course, Sasha had been secretive. She hadn't volunteered the information or given in when Romy pressed. All her sister said was that he was important. Political? Clearly, he was someone who had a lot to lose if news got out. Sasha didn't want him to be exposed either. Would it put a target on her baby's back?

"Tell me something about you that I can't read on your resume," Eric picked up the conversation. Was he trying to distract her so she would stop panicking?

Little did he know asking about her or her background sent her blood pressure up, not the other way around.

"I have no idea what my next move is going to be." It was an honest response and one she hoped would pass without a whole lot of questions.

"After selling your bakery," he confirmed.

"Yes." Relief washed over her at the change in subject away from the driver. "Don't get me wrong, I'm happy to be working where I am for now. I'm sure at some point I'll be ready for a new challenge."

"Any ideas what that might be?" Eric asked. Talking to him was easy, natural. *Dangerous.*

"I've been playing around with moving out of state and opening a bed and breakfast," she admitted.

"Your baking would probably seal the deal for most folks. They wouldn't be able to resist staying at your place," he pointed out with a smile. There was something so comforting about being with Eric.

"Until they wanted to stick around for dinner," she quipped. She'd said it jokingly but there was a lot of truth to it.

"You could always hire someone to come in for dinners," he offered.

"True. But then, it wouldn't be homey. I wouldn't be hosting anymore." It might seem like a small detail but that was the difference between staying somewhere that was okay versus somewhere that felt like home.

"The devil is in the details," he said.

"Truer words have never been spoken." A smile crept across her face despite needing to check the side view mirror every few seconds to make one hundred percent certain the SUV was gone for good. The more she thought about it, the SUV had to be a message. "I'd want the place to reflect me and my personality. Lots of fresh flowers every-where, and I'm obsessed with the smell of lavender. Does that sound like overkill?"

"Not to me," he said. "Same is true of any business. You want your name to mean something and you do that by putting your personal stamp on it. The business is an extension of you."

He really did get it.

"That's the way I look at it." Now it was her turn to ask questions. "What about you? Did you always want to be a cattle rancher?"

"From day one," he admitted.

"Your wife—"

"No wife," he countered.

"Girlfriend must not get to see you very much," she continued, ignoring the little dance in her heart with the knowledge he wasn't married.

"I just got out of a complicated relationship," he said by way of explanation. "I have no plans to jump back on that merry-go-round anytime soon."

"Oh. Sounds like a bad experience," she said.

"You could say that," he confirmed, shifting in his seat. Did the conversation make him uncomfortable?

Romy's stomach free fell at the thought this sexier-than-anyone-had-a-right-to-be man sitting next to her was single. She chalked it up to the out-of-control attraction she felt. Of course, she would be falling for a man committed to living single.

The only reason she was going down that path in the first place was because it was safe. No chance this man would try to pin her down in a relationship. Plus, he had that whole tall, dark, and handsome bit down. Despite being around him feeling like the most natural thing, it also inundated her with all kinds of sensual sensations she'd practically forgotten existed. She couldn't go there with Eric. The minute he found out why she was really there, he would turn his back on her forever at best and she didn't want to think about what might happen at worst. But could she really keep her secret and work beside this man in the coming days?

6

"Thank you for taking me to meet your mother."

"She enjoyed meeting you and the boost to her moral seemed to also lift her spirits." Eric pulled into a spot near the main house, surprised by Dawn's comment. "I'd call it a win-win."

"She was very gracious, especially under the circumstances," she said after a thoughtful pause. Then, not-so-subtly shifted the topic. "What was it like growing up here?"

"Chaotic," he said with a chuckle. "We can talk about it over lunch if you'd like to eat now."

"I would," she said, and her cheeks flushed, contrasting against creamy skin that his fingers itched to touch.

Eric forced his gaze away as he exited the truck and then circled around to grab her door for her. He held out his hand, which she took, and then leaned on him to climb down from the vehicle. More of that electricity shot through him, and for a split second, he couldn't help but wonder what it would feel like having more of her body pressed against his.

Shaking off the thought, he followed her inside the back

door to the kitchen where Prudence sat at the table feeding
Angel, who was seated in her carrier.

"Prudence, I'd like you to meet Dawn," he said. When he
glanced at the temp, he was certain he saw a look pass
behind her eyes.

"This is Angel," Prudence said with a broad smile.

"She sure looks like one," the temp said after clearing
her throat. "It's nice to meet you."

"You too," Prudence said with more of that warmth in
her voice. "This is an amazing place. I think you'll be happy
working here."

For the second time since walking in the kitchen, something passed behind Dawn's eyes.

"I'll heat up something while the two of you get to know
each other," Eric stated.

"Actually, I'd probably better eat at my desk instead. I
brought lunch and it's in the office." She couldn't back out of
the room fast enough.

"Did I say something wrong?" He looked to Prudence for
an answer because he was confused.

"Not to me," she said. "But this family can be a little bit
overwhelming to some people."

He wondered if she wanted to add the words, "like me."
She'd been one of the shiest people he'd ever met, early on,
though she'd warmed up to the family after marrying
Adam. The three of them were everything good about a
young family.

And everything Eric wanted to avoid, he thought with a
chuckle.

"Should I go see if everything's okay?" he asked, seriously feeling lost about what to do next. A growing part of
him wanted to confront her about the look he'd seen pass

behind her eyes twice now. Something was up. Was it as simple as being overwhelmed?

"I'd give her some space," she said. "Let her figure it all out for herself. This is her first day and she might need a minute to process."

"I drove to the hospital to check on our folks." Eric grabbed a ready-made meal from the fridge and then walked over to the microwave.

"How is your mom today?" Prudence asked.

"Missing her grandchild," he quipped. There was a whole lot of truth to that statement.

"Angel misses her grandmother more than any of us could probably realize. She was fussy this morning and I'm certain it was the time her grandmother normally shows up," she said.

"Kids are probably smarter than anyone gives them credit," he agreed.

"That's true." Prudence nodded. "How about your father? Any news about his condition?"

"The prognosis is good. Mom said the doctor is keeping him for observation. Wants him to stick around the hospital for a few more days. He slept the entire time I was there, which wasn't too long. I didn't want to disturb him when he needed to be gaining his strength." And then there was the whole not being big on hospitals thing. Plus, seeing his dad in a weakened condition didn't do good things to Eric. His father might heal but what would his recovering look like? Would he ever be the same?

"Sounds like good news. Doesn't seem like the doctor is too concerned about him if he's only keeping him for observation at this point," she said.

Angel made a cooing noise, causing Prudence to break

into a wide smile. The once-shy person he'd probably passed on the streets for years had truly blossomed.

From out of the corner of his eye, he saw Dawn standing in the hallway, leaning toward the kitchen. What was she doing? Was she afraid to come in?

He grabbed his plate out of the microwave and took a seat at the table, nodding toward the hallway.

Prudence seemed to catch on right away when she made eyes. "What about you? How are you holding up?"

"Me?" He made a show of being confused by the question. "I'm right as rain."

"Come on, tough guy." Prudence had been baptized by fire into the family since moving in a couple of months ago. She'd gotten up to speed real fast with all the goings on at Firebrand Ranch and, in some ways, it seemed like she'd always been here. "Be honest. How are you really?"

"Can't complain," he said. "The thought of losing Dad hit me square in the chest but it wasn't because he and I were close. It was all of a sudden like we would never get the chance to clear the air. Does that sound strange?"

"Not to me," she said, giving the baby another bite of soft food. There were all kinds of flavors, none of which could replace a steak on the grill. "And especially not after everything that has come to light in recent weeks."

"Exactly. Those and other things that reach way back. Thinking of him dying without us ever sitting down and having a one-on-one over a beer hit me," he said. "I don't know if it'll ever happen no matter how long he lives. Losing the possibility wasn't something I was ready to face."

"Makes sense," she said. "It's the most natural thing to want to be square with the people who brought us into this world."

"Except the family seems more divided than ever," he

said, realizing he probably shouldn't talk about their problems with a guest listening from the hallway. Except he couldn't rightly say he was good at making small talk and Dawn wasn't exactly a guest. She was an employee. This was what people got when they talked to him, honesty. He'd never been one for social events where everyone put on airs, pretending to be someone they weren't. He liked small affairs where people could speak their minds.

"How about Lynn?" Prudence asked without making eye contact. "Adam said she reached out to you about your dad."

Eric shrugged. "And?"

"Did you respond?" Prudence asked.

"I told her the same thing I told you. I'm fine," he said. "Told her there was no need to be concerned."

"That's fair." There was a note of concern in her voice despite the quick response.

"And what exactly does that mean?" he asked, his curiosity getting the best of him.

"It's just that your brother is worried about you," she admitted.

"He doesn't need to be," he quickly countered. Too quickly for his response to be believable he was afraid.

"This is Adam we're talking about." She laughed and rolled her eyes.

"My big brother does think he has to be responsible for all of us heathens," he teased. "He has his hands full trying to keep up with us. But he's barking up the wrong tree if he thinks I'm in a bad place."

Eric glanced at the window and saw the reflection of the temp who was still in the hallway, studying her phone like it had the answers to the bar exam and she was on her last attempt. *Interesting.*

"Well, you can tell my brother that I really am fine and

don't need him to keep watch over my shoulder. I'm not getting back together with Lynn." He said the words a little louder this time. Did some part of him want to ensure the temp heard?

ALL THIS DECEIT would eat Romy from the inside out if she didn't stop it soon. She'd had to excuse herself from the kitchen being around Prudence and Angel. There was something so pure, so innocent about the mother and baby. It didn't seem right being dishonest while in the same room with them. Then there was the fact she'd almost corrected Eric when he'd introduced her as Dawn.

Dawn Driver. That was her new name. She needed to repeat it dozens of times until it became rote.

Five more texts to Sasha. Zero responses. Something was seriously off. Romy could feel it in the pit of her stomach. She stood there, frozen to her spot in the hallway, wanting to rejoin Eric and the others in the kitchen, unable to force her feet to move.

So, she listened.

Was Lynn the relationship he'd referred to earlier? Curiosity, nothing more, had her perking up when he discussed his relationship. From what she could tell, there was a breakup or at the very least a pause.

Glancing up, she caught sight of Eric in the reflection of the window. And he was looking right at her.

Panic gripped her as her fight, flight, or freeze response kicked in. Hers had always been freeze. Everything suddenly moved in slow motion and her brain tried to catch up, but it was like walking through a field of molasses, her feet sticking to the ground with every step.

Regroup. She needed to retreat and come up with an excuse as to why she was eavesdropping.

A few seconds ticked by and neither broke eye contact. With a deep breath, she plucked up the courage to turn and dash back into the office where she reclaimed her seat. The thought of food turned her stomach right now. If there weren't red flags on her before, there had to be a few now. This was so not good. Heart pounding the inside of her ribcage, she grabbed her lunch bag, needing something to do with her hands besides twist them together.

Technically, she was still on her lunch break. Could she bolt out the front door long enough to gather herself before she had to face Eric again? If he walked through the door right now, she'd have a panic attack.

So, of course, that was exactly what happened.

"Everything okay in here?" Eric asked, stopping in the doorway.

"Yes." She pulled out an apple from her lunch bag, and then set it on top of her desk.

"You sure about that?" he asked, an eyebrow raised.

She shook her head. "No. I'm not."

Her honesty seemed to strike a chord.

"I'm a good listener." He walked inside, and then turned one of the chairs around to face her before sitting down. He leaned forward, resting his elbows on his knees, and clasped his hands together.

"It's my sister. She's gone rogue and I'm worried about her since we just found out she was pregnant." Yes, she'd just handed over a lot of information and yet if she didn't tell someone she might literally explode.

"And you've called her?" he asked after a thoughtful pause. There was so much compassion in his voice, and that was so not good for her while she was holding the line on the lie.

She nodded.

"I figured. Just wanted to cover bases," he said. "When was the last time you spoke to her?"

"Recently, but I've been texting her and she's not responding," she admitted, only a little worried she was giving up too much information. There weren't enough deep breaths in the world to fix this.

"Does she live anywhere near here?" he asked.

"Afraid not."

"So, you can't exactly pop in and check on her," he said.

"That's right."

"What if you took the rest of the day off," he said.

"It's an amazing offer. Too generous, in fact." She didn't deserve his kindness. She also couldn't believe the man was being this good to her on her first day of work. She had to be messing up big time. No, big time wasn't nearly big enough a term for how badly she was screwing up this day. And his kindness was only making matters worse. How was she supposed to walk away from the kindest family she'd met in far too long after stealing their secrets? "I can't accept it."

Eric rubbed the day-old scruff on his chin. The five o'clock shadow only added to his sex appeal, which was already more than any one person should be gifted.

"Then, what can I do to help?" he asked.

"You don't know me. Why would you do that?" She genuinely wanted to know.

"Do what?" His dark brow shot up.

"Be so kind," she said.

"I'd like you to stick around for longer than a few weeks. It looks like my dad will need more time than we originally figured, and my mom could use the break from worrying about ranch business. They leave two big holes that need to be filled. So, it's simple on my end. A happy employee sticks around," he said like it was nothing.

It was something. A huge something. So huge, in fact, that she realized she couldn't keep lying to this man. Not when she stared into those incredible green eyes of his. She checked her phone again, wishing for some kind of response from Sasha.

There was nothing. And a sinking feeling had Romy fearing the worst. This was a hole she had no idea how to dig out of on her own. And she might just end up making everything worse, except that after meeting Eric's family there was no way she could go through with this lie. There was no one she could call in order to back out of this situation. Sasha might be in real physical danger. All Romy could do was explain the situation to Eric and ask for his help.

With a deep breath, she said, "My pregnant sister is in trouble and I'm not who you think I am."

7

"Then you better start explaining." Eric had known something was up from the beginning with the new hire. Now, they were finally getting somewhere. The trick would be to stay calm no matter what surprises came next.

"My name is Romy, not Dawn, for starters," she said with a look that begged forgiveness. He'd hold judgment since he had a feeling this was only the beginning.

"Why did you lie about your name?" He kept his voice as steady as he could, figuring he'd get more information that way. Plus, he wanted to get to the bottom of this situation. Too many things didn't add up, and yet there was something about her that made him want to listen, help if he could. Was it her reaction to walking into the hospital room? Yes. He believed that was a large part of the reason. Then there was the fact she'd been scared senseless with the road rage driver. No one should be forced to feel that way, and he wanted to find out why she'd reacted in that manner. But also, it was her. He wanted to listen to what *she* had to say.

"Because I didn't want anyone to know who I was," she said. "And before you say anything, I'd like to explain."

He clamped his mouth shut, gave a slight nod for her to continue.

"The SUV was a warning." Her chin quivered and he saw real fear in her eyes. "For me."

"You knew the driver?" He couldn't see a world where she did, but he was listening.

"Not personally. But I was planted here to do a job, and I believe I was being reminded not to mess up," she explained with a look that nearly ripped his heart to pieces. He should be angry but a picture was emerging. Her sister had gotten into some kind of trouble and now Daw...Romy...was here to fix the mistake.

"As in spy on us?" He didn't like the idea one bit.

She nodded. She was being honest with him and he'd seen her in conflict all day.

"What information are you supposed to be gathering from us?" he continued.

"Anything I can get about ranch operations and the person especially wants to know about some secret clause in your grandfather's will." She put her hands up in the surrender position. "Please don't freak out or get too angry with me. I had no idea what I was getting into when I said I would do this. I don't even know who is behind the scheme but I do know my sister has been threatened."

"Her life?"

"Possibly. Then, there's the father of her baby to consider. She's been having an affair with a married man. She was scared when I last spoke to her." Romy hung her head low for a few seconds before lifting her gaze to meet his. Tears welled in her eyes, but none fell. She seemed too determined to let the floodgates open and more and more like she needed a strong shoulder to lean on. "I know how all this must sound. Too incredible to be true. It all happened so fast and I had no idea what this assignment was truly going to entail. My sister begged for my help and..." She flashed eyes at him. "She's had a complicated life."

"One that has something to do with your reaction to walking into a hospital room earlier. Am I right?" Again, he kept his voice as calm as he could despite the anger trying to bubble up to the surface—anger that someone would essentially blackmail Romy into spying on his family when they were down. The Marshall was barely gone. Eric's father wasn't released from the hospital yet. Then again, this was the perfect time to attack. Someone had been buying up property in and around Lone Star Pass. His best guess was the two incidences were linked.

"Yes," she admitted. "Strange how the mind works. I'd blocked that day out of my mind completely, forcing it from my thoughts like wiping a blackboard with an eraser. The mind blocks out traumatic events for the sole purpose of survival. Today caused the horrible memory to come crashing down and I realized I'd been remembering the whole reason my sister came to live with me wrong." She redirected her eyes, staring out the window with an unfocused gaze. "The day I saw my father crying wasn't the moment I realized my sister's home life was out of control."

Chin up, head high, she sat still for a long moment like she was gathering enough strength to continue. Then, she redirected her gaze, staring out the window.

"She was twelve years old. My father was there. He'd taken me to visit her. There were broken ribs. One side of her face was so swollen that I barely recognized her." Romy's hands fisted and he wondered if she even realized it. "A new 'uncle' as her mother made my sister call him apparently had a temper. He took it out on a child."

Romy seemed barely able to contain her emotions. Despite the betrayal, all his protective instincts flared. More than anything, he wanted to understand. He should be angry with her and yet, how could he? Hearing her reasoning made him want to help. Besides, it was her first day on the job and no harm had been done. So much about her earlier behavior made sense to him now. The over-the-top nervousness. The hesitation to talk. She clearly wasn't the kind of person who would willingly damage another person's business or family, for that matter. Hers seemed to mean everything to her.

Right now, all he could do was sit in silence and listen. She needed to be heard. There was a vulnerability in her voice, in spite of the strength she was displaying. If anything, this made him respect her even more.

Don't get him wrong, whoever was trying to hurt his family had to and would be taken down. Eric wouldn't put up with an assault on the ranch. His thoughts snapped to a dark place. One he didn't want to consider. Until recent events, this would never have crossed his mind. Now? Times were different and a question remained. Could Uncle Keif somehow be behind this?

Eric didn't want to go down that road. He tabled the idea for the time being.

"It was bad, Eric," Romy said with a voice that cracked.

"How old were you when this happened?" he asked.

"Nineteen, and on my own with a stable job," she stated. "My sister was twelve. She was practically a baby."

"Did they arrest the bastard who did that to her?" he asked, hoping that in talking about it she could finally deal with the horror of it and take away some of its hold on her.

He couldn't imagine the kind of trauma this scenario would cause for her, seeing her sister abused and feeling helpless to stop it. His family had their issues growing up, like everyone's did, but he was close with his brothers. Their dad might not have won father of the year, or husband for that matter, but he'd never physically abused any one of his kids to Eric's knowledge. Was there emotional neglect? That was a whole different story. Their mother had more than made up for an absent father and they'd had each other to lean on.

"He got a slap on the wrist as far as I'm concerned. The real damage was done to Sasha—"

Romy's eyes widened at the realization she'd just spoken her sister's name out loud.

"I'm sorry to burden you with all this," she stated. "I should just leave and face the consequences. Figure out how to save her on my own. For the record, I didn't collect any information from your family or your business. After meeting everyone, I could never do that."

He had his doubts she could do it even if she hadn't been introduced around. She'd been too twisted up about being here in the first place. Too honest. Too kind. Those traits couldn't be faked. A person who'd taken in a sibling when they were barely legal themselves then started and ran a successful business wasn't the type to play dirty with anyone.

"No harm, no foul." He meant it. To prove it, he reached over and clasped their hands together. He was starting to get used to the sizzle happening between them and the electrical current that came with contact. "I hope you won't feel bad about coming here to the ranch even though it was under the wrong circumstances. And I promise not to make you regret telling me. Thank you for doing that."

A spark of hope lit her blue eyes.

"It took a lot of courage to do what you just did," he continued. "Says a lot about your character and the kind of person you are on the inside."

"I was planning to damage your family. I don't deserve your praise." A tear spilled out of her eye, rolling down her cheek.

The temptation to reach up and brush it away with his thumb was almost too much. He stopped himself, instead saying, "You don't have to do this alone. I'm on your side now. I'm aware of what's happening, and you don't have to deal with this on your own if you don't want to. You have the power of me and all of my family's resources beside you now."

Romy blinked a couple of times like she couldn't possibly have heard him correctly.

"Why would you do that?" she asked.

"Because it's the right thing to do. Because I live by a code that says you don't kick someone when they're down. And because you don't deserve to be in a position that forces you to choose between loyalty to your sister and harming someone's business." He meant every word.

"You should hate me at this point, Eric. I came here with the intent to destroy your family business," she said.

"What would hating you accomplish?" he asked.

She shrugged.

"In my experience, when a good person does something bad, they always punished themselves more than anyone else ever could." He'd stopped getting angry about things outside of his control a long time ago.

Now was the time to get answers about who was targeting his family.

ERIC WAS RIGHT. Romy would never be able to forgive herself if she'd brought harm to such a lovely family. And now she wouldn't be able to forgive herself for the damage she was doing to her sister and the baby. She twisted her hands together, figuring this was a no-win situation. Sure, her character was still intact. But at the end of the day, what would that really get her?

"From my viewpoint, this whole situation is hopeless," she said.

"All is not lost." Eric leaned forward. His rough, strong hand covering hers kept her panic levels a notch below freak out. "We can work together to bring down the person threatening your sister and remove the threat for us at the same time."

"How on earth would we pull off something like that without getting caught?" she asked, figuring it sounded too good to be true.

"I'm not going to say it will be easy. I can feed you just enough information to stall for time as we figure this out," he reasoned.

"What about my sister? She isn't responding to any of my texts. I'm certain the SUV was a threat to me, a reminder that I need to deliver or else," she said, an overwhelming sense of panic threatening to engulf her. She wouldn't... couldn't allow it to happen.

"Ranch security needs to be made aware of a threat. I don't have to go into details and I'll ask them to keep the conversation between us for starters." His eyes sparked when he got onto a good idea. Sweet wasn't normally a word she would associate with sexy before she'd seen that look on him. He had the whole melt-her-heart thing down.

This situation was probably throwing her off her game so much because she'd worked for everything in life on her own. *Against all odds* should probably be tattooed on her body somewhere.

"I don't know." There were so many people around the ranch and the more who knew the better chance of information leaking. She trusted Eric but wasn't so sure bringing in others was a good idea. If word got out, there was no telling what would happen to Sasha. Plus, she had no idea who or how many people were involved. "It's risky, Eric."

"If there was another way, I'd be all for it. This might be our best shot. First and foremost, we need to find your sister," he said.

"I need to go to her. Check out her apartment. See if she's there and not answering," Romy said. "For all I know, she could be in the hospital. Something might have happened with the baby or..."

She didn't want to go there where the baby's father might have done something to Sasha to 'deal' with what he might view as a problem. Considering the fact he was a married man, possibly with a family, he would have a lot to lose if word got out.

"I'll drive," he said. "We should wait until it's dark and I'll borrow a different vehicle."

"Is there one without the ranch logo on it?" she asked, figuring that was how the SUV driver found her. She was safer on the ranch, but she couldn't worry about her own personal safety right now. All that mattered to her was finding Sasha and making sure nothing bad happened to her.

Romy would never forgive herself if she let her sister down.

"I can probably drum one up if you don't mind a sedan," he said.

"As long as there's no identifying sticker on it, I'd ride on the back of a motorcycle," she admitted. Not that she would like racing down the street in boots and exposed skin. No one would expect her on the back of one, least of all her sister.

"That can be arranged," he said without missing a beat.

Maybe she'd gone too far with that crack. She started to open her mouth to oppose the idea and decided against it almost as fast. "I can change into jeans so I won't have to worry about skinning my legs."

"I don't wreck." His words were spoken with the kind of certainty that left no room for doubt.

"Motorcycle it is," she confirmed, feeling a whole lot better about her choice to trust in him.

"Do you have any idea who your sister could be having an affair with?" he asked.

"No. She didn't confide in me about him. I didn't realize she was in a relationship until she told me she was in trouble," Romy admitted. "I hate to say this, because it might come off the wrong way, but she wasn't returning my calls. This happens sometimes between us. I'll reach out and not hear back from her. Sometimes a couple of months pass by before she checks in. I don't like it, but I'm used to it if that makes any sense."

"It does. Believe me, with eight brothers and nine cousins, we have all kinds of relationships going on here. I have a younger brother by the name of Fallon in the military, who I haven't talked to in ages. Family can be like that," he said with compassion.

"There are so many of you. It's just the two of us. How

hard should it be?" She felt guilty for not pushing the issue with Sasha more.

When she glanced up at Eric, she saw questions dance behind his eyes.

"It's just, I'm older than she is and I—"

"Feel responsible for everything she does." He finished the sentence for her. He wasn't wrong.

"How do you know?" She had probably been obvious but she was curious as to what his answer would be.

"It's easy to see how much you care about your sister." Again, he wasn't wrong. "I've seen this before. My older brother Adam feels the same way about us. There's something about being the oldest in a family that makes a person—"

"Feel responsible for everything." She cut him off. It was true, though. Since seeing her twelve-year-old sister in a hospital bed along with a helpless father, Romy had taken on the responsibility for her family.

"It's a nice idea and I can't fault you for it," he said.

"But?" *There always was one*, she thought.

"It's probably misguided," he said before quickly adding, "even though it comes from the heart."

Romy blew out a sharp breath. The man was probably right. And yet she couldn't change even if she wanted to. "There are times when she's still twelve years old in my eyes."

"But she's not. She's going to be a mother soon," he pointed out.

The realization struck like a physical blow. Sasha, a mother? The news was starting to sink in. "If I'm honest, I can barely imagine it."

How would her sister survive as a young mother? The thought sent a shockwave reverberating through Romy.

Would she have to step in? Did Sasha have what it would take to care for a child? Did Romy, for that matter?

She doubted it. Except that, strangely, she could see herself having a family with a partner like Eric. With someone like him by her side, she could see herself having a child...children?

The realization shocked her. Setting it aside, she hoped they could find answers at her sister's apartment.

8

The rest of the day ticked by with Romy working in the office and Eric sticking close under the guise of training. Dinner was quick and dirty, consisting of a heated meal left by the Marshall's housekeeper. Night would fall by the time they reached Austin. Eric stood at the base of the stairs, waiting for Romy to come down so they could investigate her sister's apartment.

A jogging outfit shouldn't look so good on a person. The shade of pale pink highlighted those incredible blue eyes and creamy skin.

"Try this," he said as she met him on the ground floor. He placed a baseball cap on her head. "Should make it more difficult to identify you inside the vehicle."

She took in a deep breath like she was gathering her strength. "Okay. Let's do this."

He reached for her hand and she met him halfway. Fingers linked, he walked with her out the back door near where his mother's Mercedes was parked. No identifying marks, just like Romy had requested. She was right. Even though her sister's apartment was in Austin and he highly doubted the college crowd there would identify his family's vehicles, the person blackmailing Sasha would. His mom drove an otherwise basic Polar white C-Class. Not too expensive. Not too many bells and whistles. Elegant enough for his mother's taste.

The Mercedes had been delivered to the main house by security. Eric had brought head of security Steven Paine as up to date as possible, considering most facts were on a need-to-know basis. Paine, of all people, understood. He'd spent the better part of ten years in the military before coming to work at the ranch.

Paine was still on duty when Eric drove past the guard shack. Eric waved as Romy sat quietly in the car. Thinking? Processing?

"I know I said this before, but I want to thank you for trusting me," he said. "I'm not under the impression you talk about your sister to many people."

"You're the first person I've ever spoken to about Sasha," she admitted, as he'd suspected. "And, this might sound odd under the circumstances, talking about her with you has helped me put our relationship in perspective. I'd never given much thought to how protective I am of her and why. I've been treating her like she's still that same innocent twelve-year-old. But she's not. She's a grown woman and I've done everything I humanly can to help her. I still will. It's just I understand why my need runs so deep now and why I'm willing to forgive things she shouldn't be getting away with at this age."

"I've heard boundaries with family are a good idea." He smiled as he navigated toward the highway leading to Austin. "Let me know if you get them figured out. We could use some in my family."

He smiled in an attempt to lighten the mood.

She reached over and touched his bicep, causing those familiar jolts to shoot through him. "I guess we all need a little work in that department then. I think you're telling me not to be so hard on myself."

"From what I've seen so far, you're a good person," he said. "Your love for your sister runs deep and that's admirable. In my experience, relationships are a two-way street. Believe me when I say they don't work when all the responsibility falls on one side."

From the corner of his eye, he saw that she nodded. He hoped she'd take those words to heart.

"What is the plan when we get to Austin?" she asked, shifting in her seat as she changed the subject. "Other than the obvious fact that we're going to my sister's apartment."

"We'll circle the building once. Then, go find a place to park several blocks away. If memory serves and not much has changed in the capital city, then street parking is always next to impossible anyway." He hadn't been to Austin in a while, though he couldn't imagine much had changed. With the steady influx of folks moving to Texas, and Austin in particular, traffic would only get worse.

"The terrible job of city planning on roads doesn't help," she quipped.

"That's what happens when folks decide they can stop population growth if they don't build roads to support it." He'd never understood the logic.

"Makes absolutely no sense," she agreed. "I get the whole *Build it, they will come* mantra but Austin is proof the opposite is most definitely not the case."

"Truer words have never been spoken," he said. "Neglecting infrastructure in the hopes people would stay away because there weren't enough roads clearly did not work."

"You're right about parking, though. We might be making a hike, which I don't mind," she said.

"Do you mind if I ask what happened to your sister after you saw her in the hospital?" He had a guess.

"I challenged her mother for custody and won," she said with pride that made him respect her even more.

"That couldn't have been easy for you," he noted. "Being responsible for a kid when you weren't much older yourself."

"I was nineteen with a job and an apartment that I earned on my own. I thought I knew it all and was ready to handle anything," she said. "Naturally, I was out of my league on all fronts. But we made it work."

He suspected *she* made it work. This also confirmed why she seemed to bear the burden of responsibility when it came to her sister.

"She's lucky to have you in her corner, Romy." He meant every word. He wondered if Sasha realized how much her sister put herself on the line. The fact she left Romy hanging for weeks, sometimes months on end, didn't paint Sasha in a good light.

"She'd be even luckier if I can get her out of this," she said with a hesitancy in her voice.

"We've got a good shot as long as we keep working together," he said. "Somehow, I'm not sure that's exactly what you're talking about."

"I keep cycling back to the same question...when will it end? Sure, I bailed her out of the last mess she got herself into and sacrificed in order to pay her rent when she blew the money or quit her job. There are always excuses with my baby sister." She blew out a breath it sounded like she'd been holding inside for years. "Where does it stop?"

Eric wished there was something he could do or say to help.

"I'm sorry. I don't mean to dump this on you," she quickly said, reaching over to touch him again.

"Don't be. We have a decent drive ahead of us and, besides, who would you talk to if not me?" Eric didn't add the part about *wanting* to be her support. This was the first time in his life he barely knew someone and felt such a deep connection. For reasons he couldn't explain, he wanted to be her shelter in a brewing storm. "Besides, I actually like talking to you which is rare for me."

"I'm the one doing all the talking," she said with a warm smile, "but thank you."

"Then, it's a good thing I like listening to you." More than he cared to say at the moment.

ROMY HAD ALWAYS HELD her secrets tightly to her chest.

She'd never been one to talk about personal problems with anyone else, let alone someone she'd only just met. Despite knowing Eric for a short time, she couldn't shake the feeling they'd known each other all their lives. What was the saying? Two old souls? She'd never really believed it to be true until now, until Eric. Plus, she could use a shoulder to lean on under the circumstances.

Rather than fight the urge to stop talking to him, she just let go and decided to see where it took her. Weight was already lifting, freeing her to breathe again.

"To be honest, I'm worried about Sasha's ability to care for herself if I decide to let her stand on her own two feet one day," she admitted.

"Rightfully so based on what you've told me so far. Is

your sister capable of caring for a child?" Eric asked. "Based on what I've seen with Angel, it takes a village."

"It's a fair question. She can't take care of herself, so it's highly unlikely to my thinking that she'll be responsible enough to care for another living human," Romy said. "I haven't spoken to her about what she plans to do because this all happened too quickly to process but she asked me to be a good aunt, so my guess is that she intends to keep the baby."

"She used the baby as leverage?" he asked with no judgment in his tone.

When he put it that way, it sounded much worse. He was right though.

"You're right. She did. I shouldn't want to defend her but that's exactly what's happening. I want to say she's still too young to be responsible for her actions. If she's seriously going to have a newborn depending on her for survival, Sasha needs to make big changes in her life." The realization struck Romy. So did a stab of guilt. Had she been making it a little too easy for Sasha to be irresponsible? "I keep running to her rescue but find that I want her to be able to stand on her own two feet more and more."

"It's natural to want to rescue the people we love. I would go to the ends of the earth for any one of my brothers," he said. "I can only imagine how amplified it would be for you, given the past circumstances."

"Sasha and I need to have a serious discussion about our relationship when this is all over." Romy prayed she and Eric would be able to save her sister from the mess she'd gotten herself into. "I'll always be here for her but there are going to be boundaries. She's going to have to step up and take care of herself. Her problems keep escalating. I'm not even sure I can get her out of this one."

"There are resources available if she'll accept them. Parenting classes. Counselors. If she's willing to put in the work, we'll find the right people to help," Eric said.

"You would do that for my sister? You don't even know her." Romy was blown away.

"I know you and that's good enough for me," he said.

This time when she reached over to touch his arm, he took her hand in his, and then placed a tender kiss on her palm. Warmth engulfed her, lighting a spark inside her like she'd never known. The experience threw her out of her comfort zone, one that had carefully constructed walls. Eric threatened to crash right through them and it both scared and thrilled her, opening her up to new possibilities. Romy stopped herself right there.

More than anything, she needed safety, not all-consuming blaze. With effort, she pulled her hand back and stared at her palm for a long moment as the engine idled, while the car was stopped at the red light. Emotions were heightened and that had to be the reason she felt such a draw to this man. It couldn't be attraction. Could it? This strong? The pull to him was earth to sun. Cold to flame.

The rest of the ride to her sister's apartment might have been quiet but the air sparked with electricity. The apartment itself sat near the corner of 6ᵗʰ Street and N. Lamar Blvd. The brown brick building was two stories and had six apartments total, all efficiencies. The parking lot was small. Sasha's 1990 Honda Civic was parked in the lot.

"My sister's car is here," she pointed out.

Eric slowed down on the narrow one-lane street. "Where?"

"The silver one." On closer inspection, there was something wrong with the window on the driver's side. "I can't see clearly but can you see what's going on with the driver's side window?"

"It's shattered," he said.

She gasped, fighting the urge to open the door and run over there to investigate. Being out in the open, exposing herself would be a bad idea. The jerks behind this could be watching. She sank a little lower in the seat at the thought as a group of three college students passed by with a couple coming from the opposite direction. She scanned the faces, searching for a clue one or all of them could be behind this as unlikely as that might be.

More college kids filled the street in groups of two, three, and four. She scanned the backpack-wearing, hoodie-clad young faces. There were fewer students in Austin this time of year but it seemed like many were already returning in preparation for the first day of school in a couple of weeks. Young people moved out of dorms as early as possible, renting apartments or going in on houses to lower astronomical college costs.

"I wish we could park in her lot for a few minutes. I couldn't even get a good look to see if a light was on in her apartment," she said.

"Which one is hers?" he asked.

"Second floor on the far end. There's no way to see it from the street through the trees." The oaks were in full bloom so no ability to see through the leaves. "Do you think they'll be watching her apartment?"

"Anything is possible," he said and there was a note in his voice that made her uncomfortable.

"You don't think she's here, do you?" she asked.

He shook his head.

"Do you still think we should check?" She wasn't sure sticking around was productive.

"We might as well since we're here," he said.

"The car window. It isn't a good sign, is it?" she asked.

"We don't want to jump to any conclusions, but no, I don't think it is," he said.

A knot formed in her chest. Her instincts were telling her the same thing. "Where should we park?"

"Away from here," he said as he glanced around the street. His serious tone was a stark reminder of the dangers they faced.

"Okay, let's get away from here then," she said.

Eric drove several blocks and made more turns than she could keep up with as he navigated around the narrow streets. She thought it was good they were in his mother's Mercedes versus his truck because she couldn't imagine navigating these narrow roads in a bigger vehicle. It was strange the thoughts she had when she was under this much pressure. She shouldn't be concerning herself with how wide the streets were when her sister was clearly in more trouble than Romy realized. First, there was the fact that Sasha hadn't responded to messages. Normally, that might not be strange, but it was out of place considering Romy was trying to save her sister's rear end. Sasha should be in near-constant contact with Romy. Then there was the simple fact she wasn't reaching out to Romy, either. Plus, the broken car window.

But what did it all really mean?

Romy was doing what was asked of her, at least as far as the jerks behind the blackmail scheme knew. They couldn't possibly realize Romy had come clean with Eric. No one knew. Eric would never share the news, except with his head of security, and that was only to keep everyone on the ranch safe. There was so much to love about being on the ranch, and the Firebrands were the most genuine and down-to-earth people she could ever meet. Who would target them? And why?

The word *greed* came to mind. Wasn't that one of the top motives for murder? She shuttered at the thought.

"Maybe we've been looking at this all wrong," she said. "I've been looking at this from the perspective of who my sister was dating and what that person had to hide. Maybe we should be looking at this from the point of view of who wants to damage your family the most."

Eric nodded. "I've been thinking along the same lines for the last half of the drive here."

The fact their minds were in sync didn't slow her growing attraction to him—an attraction that felt a lot like it was simmering into what might become an out of control forest fire if left unchecked.

But what if she ran toward the flame instead of away?

9

Eric surveyed the foot traffic on the street. There was no obvious threat there. Of course, it would help if he knew who he was looking for. He guessed a male purely based on assumptions. Potentially someone strong enough to abduct or subdue a woman. The father of Sasha's child?

In his years of experience being with and around ranch hands, he'd become good at telling a person's honesty by looking into their eyes. But whoever was targeting his family was in the shadows. What did the person intend to do with information gathered by Romy? Blackmail? It was a fearful move in his estimation. For now, the person behind this didn't want to show their hand.

"There are probably a handful of people with enough capital to challenge our ranch. The known list is short. As far as personal enemies, none of us were close to the Marshall. He pitted his sons against each other. If that doesn't paint a picture of a man, I don't know what does," he said.

"Sounds like he could have quite a few folks gunning for his business once he…"

Romy twisted her hands together instead of finishing the sentence. It was easy to guess what her next words might be.

"He might, with a reputation like his. Then, there's the fact my father and uncle are constantly at odds," he confirmed. "Considering the person behind this wants to know the details of the will and what the secret is, this is a clear if indirect attack. The sharks are circling, and they didn't wait long."

"Once we make sure my sister is safe, we can make a shortlist of names. It'll give us a starting point at the very least," she said.

He nodded, searching for a good spot to park. The dark street was perfect cover despite the rough-looking neighborhood. He circled a street five blocks away before finding an opening. Parking was nothing compared to locating a spot. The Mercedes was much smaller than he was used to driving. Navigating between two compact cars was easy.

"Keep it as low as possible. Okay?" Looking over at Romy, he tapped the bill of his ballcap until the inside rim touched his eyebrows.

"Got it." She did the same as he made his way around to the passenger side of the vehicle to open her door.

She took the hand he offered and smiled. Their eyes met, causing a bomb to detonate inside his chest. When she pushed up to her tiptoes, he met her halfway. Their lips barely touched, but he wouldn't know it from the sheer amount of electricity and heat pulsing through him at contact.

The shuffle of footsteps behind him barely registered over the whoosh-sound in his ears and the frantic beating of his heart. The blow to the back of his head with something that felt a whole lot like a tire iron shocked him back to reality. The fall from cloud nine was abrupt and harsh. His head pounded, feeling like it had actually split in two. The blunt metal instrument—a tire iron?—nearly cracked his skull in two.

"Go back inside the vehicle and call 911. Okay?" He pressed the key fob inside the flat of Romy's palm before turning around to face his enemy.

There were two men. Both large, linebacker style. Both muscled from what he could tell underneath their sweatshirts. Both wearing ski masks in August. The set dead gray eyes staring at him sent a chill right through him. This guy meant business. Before Eric could drop down and reach for the Sig Sauer in his ankle holster, he was dealt another blow. This time, from the second guy standing to his right. This time, from a wooden baseball bat. This time, dropping him to his knees as blood trickled down the side of his face.

More than anything, he wanted to hear the sound of the car door closing behind him. He didn't. Instead, he felt Romy reaching for the gun that must be exposed. His best chance, correction *their* best chance, at survival was to draw attention to him and away from Romy.

"Who are you and what do you want?" Eric needed to stall. His heft was enough to block Romy as she must have crouched down behind him.

He blinked his eyes a couple of times and gave a little headshake to try to stop the spinning. At this rate, he was going to lose consciousness and blackout, leaving Romy on her own to deal with these men. There was no way he could allow that to happen despite the tug toward darkness.

Guy One leered at Eric. Even through the mask, the guy's intention was clear. Damage Eric. Possibly even kill him?

If the two guys wanted revenge, wouldn't they take it?

"Your wallet," Guy Two said.

Eric waved a hand behind his leg to stop Romy. If all the guys wanted was money, Eric could hand over his wallet and make this go away. No problem. He reached inside his back pocket and tossed it a few feet in front of him, fighting every instinct he had to make a move when Guy One bent over to pick it up. Guy Two was still there, waiting with the bat. He could miss Eric with the next swing and hit Romy by accident instead.

No way Eric would allow that to happen. Not as long as he was conscious. Darkness was tugging at him again and he couldn't afford to allow it to suck him under.

Guy One stood up. He grabbed all the cash out of Eric's wallet, a couple hundred dollars, and then threw the leather wallet at Eric's chest. He kept his hands by his side, open, so he wouldn't provoke the guys further. If this was all they wanted, they needed to be gone.

Guilt stabbed at him for letting his guard down. What if this had been the folks behind the blackmail? They wouldn't take his money and run. They were after far more than that. They wouldn't leave witnesses.

Guy One drew his fist back like he was going to throw a punch. Nausea was kicking in at this point, bile burning the back of Eric's throat. Blood was more than a trickle down the side of his face now. Dizziness engulfed him.

It took everything inside Eric not to fight back. Letting these two walk all over him wasn't in his nature. But Romy's safety was more important than his pride.

The guys took off running, laughing.

"Let's get you inside the car," Romy said as she clicked the door lock on the key fob.

"I let you down," he ground out, as he planted a hand on the trunk of the tree next to him. The other held onto Romy.

"You couldn't," she said as darkness threatened like storm clouds rolling in. She bent down to pick up his wallet.

With effort and help from Romy, Eric managed to slide into the passenger seat. Using the control to the right on the seat, he lowered the chair to a reclining position. Halfway down, he blacked out.

BODY SHAKING FROM ADRENALINE, Romy managed to navigate onto the main roadway. She was familiar with this area of town thanks to her sister's apartment. Clearly, it was dangerous. Her sister couldn't bring up a baby here. Maybe Sasha could move in with Romy again. Then again, she still had no idea if the dad would want to have any involvement with the child or offer financial support.

Thinking too far into the future hurt Romy's brain. With a deep breath, she reminded herself to focus on the here and now. Trying to figure out more than that would only cause her to stress.

Eric was hurt and she had no idea how bad it was. She needed to get him to an urgent care facility or ER. If memory served, there was an urgent care a few blocks from her sister's apartment.

There was a surprising amount of traffic for this time of night. She thumped the pad of her thumb against the steering wheel, willing the red light to change. Blood stained his shirt.

A knot formed in her stomach at the thought of how bad this might be. It was impossible not to blame herself for his condition. And yet, she realized he would balk at the thought.

"Come on, light. Turn," she said under her breath like saying the words could somehow make it true.

When it did change, she mashed the gas pedal, speeding to the urgent care facility, praying it was still open. Her plan in the next few minutes—and that was all she would allow herself to focus on—was to get medical attention for Eric first and foremost and then call in the law.

Thankfully, the medical facility was open. She pulled up to the all-glass double doors, waving frantically. A male nurse came running out as she rolled down the passenger window.

"We were robbed a couple of blocks from here. My friend was hit in the head with a tire iron and then with a baseball bat." The words rushed out of her mouth even though time seemed to slow to a crawl. If he'd been hit in the head with both, it could very easily have turned into a critical injury.

The next thing she knew, the male nurse had the door open and was trying to rouse Eric. His head rolled from side to side like a doll's. Not a good sign.

"My name is Taft and I'll be taking care of..."

"Eric Firebrand," she supplied.

"It's my job to take care of Eric and I promise to get him back up and running as soon as possible." Taft must have noticed the panic in her eyes and she was certain it came across in her voice as well. Had to. There was no covering this level of concern. "How are you doing?"

"Me? I'm good. No one touched me," she said.

Taft flicked a small flashlight, forcing one of Eric's eyes open. He waved an arm in the air, and within a few seconds a team rolled a wheelchair out of the double doors that opened with a swish.

"We're going to take Eric inside where he'll be more comfortable," Taft said. "What's your name?"

"I'm Romy," she supplied, trying to speak over the sounds of her heartbeat pounding in her ears.

"Okay, Romy. We're going to take real good care of your friend Eric," Taft said. He stood around five feet nine inches with stacked muscles. He had dark hair and eyes, olive skin. There was a genuine caring to his voice but all she could think about right now was Eric's condition.

"How bad is it?" she asked.

"We're going to take the best care of him," Taft reassured, stepping aside to allow two others to help move Eric into the wheelchair.

"I have to call the police and report the robbery," she said.

"Why don't you pull up into a parking spot, come inside the lobby, and help yourself to something to drink. Cherie will check you in. You can call the police once you're inside," Taft said.

She nodded. Once Eric was wheeled inside, she did as Taft said. On her way into the building, she called 911.

The call was short and to the point. The operator was efficient and promised an officer would arrive in less than five minutes.

Romy walked into the lobby that was painted in cool tones. She walked straight up to the receptionist, said her name, and gave the quick and dirty rundown of what just happened.

"That's scary," Cherie said, holding up a clipboard with a stack of papers and a pen. "And a little too close for comfort."

Romy couldn't agree more. All the more reason to get Sasha and her baby out of this area of town. All Romy's warning signals flared thinking about Sasha being left alone to raise a child. But her disappearance was the most troubling.

Going down this undercover path had been the worst of bad ideas. There just hadn't been any time to think and the need to save Sasha, again, had overruled Romy's better judgment.

She could only hope there were clues as to Sasha's location at the apartment. A piece of her wanted to tell the cop everything going on, ask for an escort to her sister's apartment so she could immediately roll up her sleeves and find answers. Except doing so would mean leaving Eric alone at the urgent care, a thought she couldn't begin to fathom. The other problem was that she had no idea what it would mean to Sasha if the police were involved. She had no idea what kind of network she was dealing with. Was one person responsible? More? Were others hired? She had no idea how any of this worked and figured real life blackmail was probably nothing like what happened in the movies.

"Ma'am," Cherie said with a concerned look.

"Sorry." Romy took the clipboard.

"Take your time," Cherie said.

"Any chance I can fill this out back there?" She motioned toward the door that would allow her to access Eric's room.

"I'm sorry. Your..." Cherie's gaze dropped to Romy's left hand before she continued. "Boyfriend is most likely with the doctor right now. I promise someone will come get you as soon as they can."

Correcting Cherie probably wouldn't do any good. Boyfriend wasn't the right word to describe what was happening between Romy and Eric. Friendship didn't seem right either. A voice in the back of her mind picked that moment to throw out the word special. He was special to Romy. What did it matter? They would be together long enough to get through this...*ordeal*...and then what? They would go their separate ways. She would figure out her next move, which most likely would involve figuring out a business she could start with Sasha. Her sister would need an income better than part-time.

She thanked Cherie before taking a seat and starting on the stack of paper. The first question that stumped her? Patient date of birth.

Glancing down the page, she realized how little she knew about a man her heart decided it was falling for. Impossible, she decided. This was nothing more than an out-of-control attraction. Eric Firebrand had sex appeal to spare. He was her knight in shining armor during one of the most difficult times of her life. The attraction was all spark and no substance.

And yet, her heart argued the opposite. There was a lot of substance and she did know the man underneath the Stetson. He was honest and honorable. There was no reason in the world for him to help her. He could have kicked her out of his family home and off the ranch the minute she told him why she was really there. He hadn't so much as raised his voice when she'd said she was there to betray him. He'd understood when she explained the position she had been placed in.

Then there was her sister. He volunteered to personally help find resources for Sasha. He'd offered no judgment, only understanding and compassion, which was something she hadn't felt in far too long. For the first time in her life, she didn't feel alone when it came to figuring out a plan for her sister.

Eric had introduced Romy to several of his family members, even taken her to the hospital so she could meet his mother. Lucia Firebrand was both kind and strong, traits Romy wished to display in her own character.

A wet splotch stained the paperwork as the glass doors swished open. She glanced up through blurry eyes as an officer walked in. She brought her hand up to wave him over despite the fact she was the only one in the waiting area at this time of night. She would never know how the doc-in-a-boxes on practically every corner stayed in business when she rarely ever saw cars parked in their lots.

Romy set the clipboard down on the empty seat next to her and stood up. The officer, who was five-feet-five-inches with brown eyes, black hair pulled off her face in a ponytail, and the body of a CrossFit instructor walked to Romy.

"My name is Officer Ramirez," the officer said. "Start from the beginning and tell me what happened."

Romy explained the events as they'd gone down. Her statement didn't take more than a few minutes. "It all happened so fast."

Officer Ramirez nodded before relaying the information on the radio strapped on her left shoulder. When she was finished, she met Romy's gaze.

"Everything you've told me will help us find the men responsible," she said with compassion. "Unfortunately, these two have been around the city for a couple of weeks and we're doing our best to find them in order to keep our citizens safe. People like you coming forward helps us figure out their patterns so we can anticipate where they might strike next."

"Thank you, Officer." Being a help was good, but her thoughts kept cycling back to how Eric was doing on the other side of that wooden door.

"If you'll excuse me, I need to speak to the receptionist," Officer Ramirez said.

"Of course." Romy stared down at the paperwork. She could look up the ranch address but there was no way she could answer the other questions. Hold on a minute. She'd dropped his wallet inside her purse, figuring he might need it once they got inside the building. His driver's license would have his date of birth. And then there was his insurance card.

Maybe she could fill out the forms after all. Romy tucked a loose tendril of hair behind her ear and reached inside her handbag. She pulled out his leather wallet and checked his ID. October twenty-ninth. Eric's birthday was two days before hers.

Romy scribbled down the date on form number one. Maybe she could learn a little more about the man her heart was falling for.

10

Eric blinked through blurry eyes. He brought his hand up to a pounding head, felt a bandage.

"Hey there," came a male voice. "Welcome back."

His fight, flight, or freeze response kicked in but his body refused to cooperate despite the rush of adrenaline that caused his pulse to kick up a few notches.

"I'm Taft and I'm your nurse today."

Eric's skull hurt as he tried to nod. The reason came back to him. The robbery.

"Can you tell me where it hurts?" Taft asked.

Eric pointed to his head and blinked his eyes a couple more times. A fuzzy figure started coming into focus. He was reminded of the last time he used a real camera instead of the one on his phone and had to manually adjust the lens. The target came in and out of focus until he found the right setting. That was basically him right now.

"Anywhere else?" Taft asked.

He shook his head. Big mistake. Blinding pain shot

through his skull and down the base of his neck. Pain wasn't his top priority. "Romy?"

"Your girlfriend is in the waiting room," Taft said. "An officer is waiting to speak to you the minute you feel up to it."

"Romy." All he could seem to manage to speak was one word.

"I can go get her," Taft relented with a smile.

Eric nodded. More of that pain slammed into him with movement. He was going to have one helluva headache for days from the assault. Guilt wracked him at letting Romy down, though. He'd gotten momentarily lost in the feel of her lips—lips he could taste now when he thought about her—and lost focus. She could have been killed.

He acknowledged how lucky he'd gotten to be the target of men who wanted cash instead of the ones who were after her. He'd crossed a line that could have cost both their lives. Blood rushed in his ears at the thought of losing Romy, at the thought of his mistake costing her life. Anger fired him up as his fists clenched.

Make no mistake about it, he wouldn't be falling down that trap again, even if it meant keeping her at a safe distance, despite how much he wanted to do just the opposite. Plus, there was the obvious fact he had just set back their investigation. Anything could be happening to her sister right now and he would always wonder how much his mistake cost them. If he'd been more aware, could he have avoided the robbery and saved her sister's life? Forget about the fact a pregnancy was involved. Eric could never forgive himself if he caused Romy the kind of pain that came with losing a sister and her baby.

Granted, Romy was one of the strongest people he'd ever met. She was certainly refreshing. He hadn't been on a date in longer than he could remember that made him want a second, let alone spend a whole evening talking to someone. He got uncharacteristically chatty when Romy was in the room.

"I'll be right back." Taft stopped what he was doing at the computer.

At least Eric could see the nurse clearly now. Taft winked before walking out of the room, and then returned a few moments later with a very worried-looking Romy. A female cop came in on Romy's heels.

"How do you feel?" Romy asked. The stress cracks on her forehead outlined the fact that she'd been worried. He hated being the one to put them there when he was supposed to be her support.

"Never better." He tried to sit up. Another big mistake. He winced.

"Don't move," she said, rushing to his side. When she reached for his hand and their fingers connected, one word came to mind...*home.*

There was no way he was breaking the lifeline even though he told himself it couldn't happen again.

The officer spoke to Taft, giving him and Romy a few seconds of privacy.

"I'm sorry," he whispered.

"For what?" Concern drew her eyebrows together.

He shook his head, figuring this wasn't the time to explain why he needed to pull back from her. Based on her grip, there was no way she was letting go of his hand anyway. And, to be honest, the idea didn't appeal to him either.

The officer made her way over, interrupting the moment happening between them. She introduced herself and he gave a statement. The memory of the masked men burned into his mind. Learning they weren't the first couple targeted by the criminals didn't help his mood or his ego. He should have been watching out for dangers. He'd been lulled into a sense of security on the dark street. When he really thought about it, the situation was perfect for a crime like this one to occur. A couple in an embrace, distracted. How much of easy pickings was that?

"Thank you for your time." The officer handed over her card. "In case you remember anything else."

Eric palmed it and promised to use it if he saw the two men again. He had no plans to and lightning rarely ever struck twice in the same spot. Driving a Mercedes probably made it seem like they had money. At least the crooks hadn't made off with Eric's wallet. They'd stuck to the cash. They were small-time thugs.

Still. Anger burned through him that he let his guard down enough to allow it to happen in the first place. More than his pride was wounded. His head felt like a bomb went off inside and his injuries would hamper their investigation.

The officer excused herself as Romy took a seat on the side of the examination table. The thing was flatter than a two-by-four and his slightest move caused the paper covering to crinkle. At least the pillow underneath his head was soft.

"We need to go," he said to Romy.

"Not until you can sit up without passing out," she warned.

"I'm good. All I need is a little ibuprofen." Ibuprofen and Vicks Vapor Rub were his mother's two favorite remedies. According to Lucia Firebrand, those were the only supplies anyone ever needed in their medicine cabinet. She pretty much believed they would fix any ailment.

Trying to sit up caused more of that pain to explode in

his head but he refused to wince this time. He eased out a slow breath, like a release valve, and made it.

"See. I'll be fine." Dizziness tried to convince him otherwise. "We need to check on your sister's apartment. This is a small setback."

Romy's blue eyes took him in, and his heart squeezed at the look she gave him.

"I won't risk you getting hurt," she said with determination that said arguing was a bad idea. He added the word *fierce* to her list of good traits. She didn't need to say another word for him to realize she would do anything and everything for someone she loved, especially if that person was injured or vulnerable in some way.

Eric hadn't met a person like her in a long time. Experience told him that he wasn't likely to encounter someone like her again in this lifetime. His respect and admiration for her grew by the minute. Every conversation, every time she revealed a new layer of herself made him realize how much he was going to regret having to push her away. Because he could also see how much it was taking her to trust him in the first place. Her trust was fragile and giving it didn't come easily to someone who had had to look out for herself much of her life.

Right now, he couldn't bring himself to pull away from her. All he could do was stand near the light that was Romy and pray that it didn't shatter him into a thousand tiny flecks of dust when the time came for him to take a stand.

Where did they go from here?

∽

ROMY EXCUSED herself so she could speak to the nurse in

private. Taft stepped out into the hallway and leaned a shoulder against the wall.

"How bad is it? Really?" she asked the nurse.

"He has stitches and a mild concussion," he informed. "I wish I could force him to go to the hospital, if only so they could strap him to a bed. I don't get the impression he's the type who will go home, put his feet up, and take it easy for the next week."

Guilt slammed into her because he would be pushing himself to help her when he should go home. "No, he isn't. Is there anything you can give him to knock him out for a few days?"

"I'm afraid not," Taft said.

The thought of going it alone without Eric nearly knocked her feet out from underneath her. How had she come to depend on someone she barely knew so much in such a short time? *The heart knows.*

"Even if I could get him back home on the ranch, I highly doubt he'd listen to medical advice," she said. He wasn't the lay around type. He'd be bored in half an hour, and probably unable to sit still. "What's plan B?"

"There is none. The doctor will give anti-nausea meds to give relief there. Dr. Zayne won't want to give anything for pain until the headache goes away," Taft said with an apologetic smile. "The best thing you can do for the person inside that room is get him to bed and force him to stay there at least for the rest of the night. See how he feels in the morning after a good breakfast. He's young and strong. He might surprise us all by bouncing back after a good sleep. I've heard stranger things."

"Okay. I'll keep an eye on things and see where we are tomorrow," she said with a small smile.

"No screens tonight, that includes TV. Best to keep him

in a dimly lit room. Short walks are okay but keep an eye on him in case he gets dizzy," Taft added. He pulled a sheet from a folder on the door. "This will explain everything you need to know for aftercare."

Romy took the piece of paper and thanked the nurse.

"When can he leave?" she asked, figuring he was probably already trying to move.

"We're working on his discharge paperwork now." Taft smiled. "Try not to worry too much. He'll be fine in a few days. Maybe sooner."

She nodded, appreciating the reassurance and hoping he wasn't being overly optimistic.

"Go on in and I'll be back in a few with a wheelchair," Taft urged.

Romy did as requested. The minute she opened the door, she saw Eric sitting up, legs over the side of the exam table, hands gripping the vinyl edge.

"I think they want you to lie down," she said to him.

"I'm sure they do," he said with a devastating smile. "What else did they say?"

"That I should get you to bed as soon as humanly possible." She heard how that sounded coming out of her mouth and put her hand in the air. "I wasn't saying…"

"Too bad," he quipped.

The devilish smile on his face caused her to laugh. She couldn't help it. Eric was more than just easy on the eyes. The man was hotness on a stick. He was also intelligent, and she could see a sense of humor in there, despite the circumstances. He was passionate about his work, and his family. The man was the total package and had the ability to melt her heart with a smile.

"Taft is on his way with a wheelchair," she said, needing to change the subject.

"I'm not leaving in one of those," he said, shaking his head. "Believe it or not, I'm already feeling better. I just needed a minute or two to shake off those blows."

"You have a few stitches, so we'll need to take care of those," she said.

"Right. Those. A little antibiotic ointment and I'll be fine." His smile was ear-to-ear now.

"What?" she asked.

"I finally did something my mother can't cure with Vicks Vapor Rub or ibuprofen." He laughed and, this time, winced with the movement.

"Don't hurt yourself," she said as he reached out to her. She moved by his side.

"Mind if I lean on you?" he asked.

"About time you did," she said before she could reel the words back in. They were true. He'd been a rock for her today and it was high time she returned the favor.

"Let's get out of here," he said.

"The receptionist is going to want us to check out. Taft is going to fuss at you," she reminded.

"Then, let's go before they catch up to us," he quipped. "I'll call with a credit card to cover the bill."

"Are you sure about this?" she asked.

"Positive." He sounded convincing.

"Okay then," she said on a sigh. Arguing didn't seem like it would do any good. If she refused to help, he would most likely try to walk out by himself.

This way, she could stabilize him as he walked. And she did as they slipped out the side door and toward the Mercedes.

Once she got him settled in the passenger seat, she asked, "Where to now?"

"I'm guessing you'll be the one to ream me out if I say to your sister's apartment," he pointed out.

"You're not wrong there." She left no room for doubt in her tone.

"The drive home is too far to turn back around and drive tomorrow. Would getting a hotel be okay with you? We could get adjoining rooms if—"

"My apartment is here but someone could be watching it. There's no need to be in separate rooms. I trust you, Eric." She did too. "Plus, if you try any monkey business I know where you're hurt. I'll make it worse."

For a split-second, he didn't seem to realize she was kidding as silence permeated the sedan. Then, he broke into another one of his devastating smiles.

Laughing broke up some of the tension. She not only appreciated it but needed it. There was only so much stress someone could take in a day before cracking.

"There's a Four Seasons downtown," Eric said before a thoughtful pause. "But they'll recognize me there. I'd rather fly under the radar."

"Plus, there's no need for such a fancy room for one night," she said. She'd never stayed in such an expensive place.

"You deserve a nice bed, Romy."

"There's a boutique hotel in the Warehouse district for half the price," she said after a quick check on his phone.

"Can I take a look?" he asked.

"Taft said no screen time for you. In fact, you should probably put on sunglasses," she said. "Light can trigger an even worse headache."

"Seems impossible, but I'll take your word for it," he acquiesced. He opened the glove box and produced a pair of Ray-Bans. The look worked for him after he put them on.

"Boutique hotel it is. I've never been considered trendy before. We'll see what that's like."

"You're far too classic to be a trend," she said with a smile.

He reached over to take her hand and seemed to stop himself midway.

"We should go," he said, and it was like a curtain came over his features and she could no longer read him.

What just happened?

11

"Looks like we made it."

Eric opened his eyes at the announcement. Romy had been right about one thing. Bright lights were bad, and his headache didn't need to get worse.

"I'll just run in and grab a room," she said, pulling under the canopy.

He put his arm up over his glasses to block as much of the light as possible.

"Should I find a place to park somewhere there's less light?" she asked as a valet ran over to the driver's side.

"No. No. I'll be fine." He had no idea if that statement was true but intended to force it by sheer will. Eric Firebrand could be stubborn when he wanted to be and even when he didn't. It was a Firebrand family trait that served well when applied correctly and spiraled to a quick demise when not. This time, his ox-like determination would be put to good use.

The valet stood at the ready.

"May as well both get out here. We don't exactly have any luggage," he pointed out.

"Fair point," she relented as the valet opened her car door.

She came around to the passenger side as Eric got out on his side. Standing made him feel like he'd just had three shots of tequila, despite only ever having had the occasional cold beer on a warm Saturday afternoon after taking care of outside chores.

He took the hand being offered, leaning on Romy. She might be smaller than him by a longshot, but she provided enough balance to keep him from walking like he'd just taken those tequila shots. The bandage on his forehead would explain his wobbly stance to anyone who had eyes. Eric didn't like the feeling of being out of control of his body.

"Steady," Romy said quietly as they walked to the front desk.

The bright lights hit hard, so he was relieved to have a room key within a couple of short minutes. He allowed Romy to use her personal credit card because his name was news. As soon as they got into the room, he told her that he was covering this one.

"You don't have to pay for a hotel room to stay in a city you don't even want to be in," Romy said, helping him ease onto the king-sized bed.

"Who said I don't want to be here with you?" he asked, forcing a smirk.

"You don't *have* to. I do," she said. "I can't let you pay."

"I'm the reason we're here in the first place and not inside your sister's apartment finding answers," he said straight out. "I got lost in the...when we kissed, and let you down."

The look she gave threatened to crumble his defenses.

"I was in that moment too. I was just as much to blame

as you for what happened," she said. "The real truth is that you couldn't possibly let me down. You don't even have to be here with me. You're risking your reputation, your life to help. You're keeping my secret, which can't be easy considering you're very close to your family."

"They don't need the stress right now," he admitted. After careful consideration on the ride over, he realized just how determined the person behind this must be. "Being a member of my family this summer hasn't been the easiest for anyone. There's been more change in the past few months than in the past decade. Honestly, I'd like to keep as much of this under the radar as possible until we figure out who is behind it. Someone is using your family to get information about us. How they plan to use it is anyone's guess. My guess is that they won't stop here and I have no idea what they'll try next. The quicker we figure out who is behind this, the better as far as I'm concerned."

"Thinking about all this is only going to hurt your head tonight." Her voice soothed places in his heart that had been long neglected. He was still reeling from the loss of his grandfather, his father's hospitalization, and other events in recent months. His family might be sticking together but there were days when it felt like they were all hanging on by a thread. And that was before his father's heart attack.

Eric toed off his boots and eased back onto the mountain of pillows stacked behind him. He reached back and repositioned a couple of them to make himself more comfortable.

"How about water?" she asked.

"I can—" He tried to move but winced.

"I'm already up. It's right here," she said, moving to the pair of courtesy bottles on the counter. She opened one and brought it over, holding it out. Once again, when he took the offering their fingers grazed. The familiar electricity comforted him now. The sizzle heated the tips of his fingers. This probably wasn't the right time to let his imagination run wild, except that was exactly what happened. "Is everything okay?"

He looked up to find her studying him.

"Never better," he said.

"What can I do?" She twisted her hands together.

"Sit down. Relax. Drink water with me. We aren't going anywhere tonight. You might as well get comfortable," he pointed out.

"A shower sounds like heaven to me right now," she said.

"By all means, take one."

"Brushing my teeth sounds amazing too." She frowned. "But I don't have a toothbrush available."

"Call down to the front desk," he said. "They'll bring up a toiletry set. Probably even throw in a razor."

"Clean clothes would be nice, but that's definitely asking too much," she said.

"Start with the call downstairs." He took a sip of water. Thinking did make his brain hurt. He could possibly push through the fog and focus, besides, the headache was already better than it had been half an hour ago. He'd take any improvement he could get.

Romy made the call, located an oversized bathrobe, and then sat at the foot of the bed and waited.

"Can I ask about your family?" He wanted to know more about her.

"Ask anything you want." She leaned forward.

"You've talked about your sister, obviously. You've mentioned your father. But you haven't said anything about your mother. Is she in the picture?" he asked, hoping the question wasn't out of bounds.

"Oh. Her," Romy said and that didn't sound too encouraging. She shrugged. "It's weird because obviously she raised me. I grew up under her roof. She and my dad were together at one point, married."

"But you two don't talk now?" he asked.

"We have this strange social media relationship," she said. "I guess once I turned eighteen she decided her job was done. She wasn't a bad mother particularly. We had a roof over our heads. She kept the lights on. There was always food on the table. We're just...different."

"How so?"

"We want different things in life. I think she always wanted to find someone to take care of her, if that makes sense. She wanted to spend her days getting her nails done, being taken out to dinner. She definitely didn't want to cook and clean. I did most of that anyway, once I got old enough, since she worked the evening shift at the hospital at patient intake," she continued.

"And you didn't fit into the picture?"

"Guess not. Like I said, now we have these strange social media interactions where she occasionally comments on a post. I can't remember the last time she called on my birthday, but she always posts on my wall," she said and there was a hint of sadness, of loss, in her voice.

"What about you? Do you want to have a closer relationship with her?" he asked.

"I should probably say yes to this question, but I accepted the situation a long time ago," she said. "Is there a part of me every once in a while that wishes I had a real mother? A mother like yours? Absolutely. There's no question. But sitting around feeling sorry for myself because I don't has never been an option."

"That's a brave stance to take," he said. He couldn't say

most would have such a good attitude about what sounded like a lackluster mother.

"I stopped expecting more from her a long time ago," she continued. "I don't know if it's being brave or just realistic."

"Does she seem happier now?" he asked.

"Kind of. But then everyone's life looks better on social media, right?" She tilted her head and gave a small smile, lighting a dozen campfires inside his chest.

This woman deserved the moon. He couldn't imagine a mother being anything but proud of her. But then, he'd seen other parents who hadn't inherited a nurturing gene. His aunt wasn't the warm-and-fuzzy type, so he knew not all mothers were cut from the same cloth. Then there was his own father to consider. The man didn't have a nurturing bone in his body. Eric's mother seemed to love motherhood.

Lucia Firebrand never hid the fact she had wanted a daughter badly. Don't get him wrong, she loved her boys with every fiber of her being. And yet, she'd never made a secret of wanting a girl. He always figured the bond was different, somehow closer.

Either way, not everyone who became a parent was cut out for the job. Something told him Romy would be an amazing mother. If the way she watched over her sister was any indication, he had no doubt.

A KNOCK at the door interrupted Romy's conversation with Eric.

"Hold on a sec," she said, lifting a finger to indicate she'd be right back. Talking to Eric was easy. He was a good conversationalist, so she was surprised to hear he didn't normally like talking.

She answered the door, took the supply packs, and then set them on the counter inside the bathroom on her way back to the bed. Eric's eyes were closed, and she hoped that meant he was resting. As she turned to walk toward the bathroom, he reached out and clasped their fingers. For a split-second, she thought he might be awake. He made a face and then turned onto his side.

Romy slipped her fingers out of his, and then placed his hand on his side before heading into the bathroom. Her shower was quick and hot. The hotel's bathrobe was soft and extended all the way down to the floor. Brushing her teeth was amazing. Being clean felt like heaven.

After checking the cell in her handbag, with no luck, she dimmed the lights further and slipped underneath the covers. A strong arm searched for her before pulling her against him. Her heart skipped a few beats as she settled in next to him, the weight of his arm over her provided an amazing amount of comfort. Breathing in his spicy male scent filled her senses.

Under normal circumstances, she could stay like this for days. Now, she couldn't stop thinking about her family. Talking about her mother wasn't normally something she did with anyone. And yet, there was something about Eric that eased more of the pain. Was her relationship with her mother hurtful? The short answer was yes. Did she wish there was more to it than the occasional social media post? Of course. But she'd figured out a long time ago that acceptance was far better than trying to force her mother to fit into an ideal. The whole square peg in round hole analogy came to mind because it exactly described their relationship. For some, being left alone as an adult and not nagged by their mother might be a blessing. But Romy had always wanted more. She wanted to be closer to her mother.

Romy was also starting to realize just how much she was trying to be more for Sasha. Her sister had been in an even worse boat that Romy, so she'd never allowed herself to feel sorry for her own situation. It was good to keep perspective —she'd come to the realization every family was built differently a long time ago—but perhaps it had stopped her from realizing that it was okay for her to be sad for her own upbringing as well.

Then, there were the Firebrands. From the outside, they probably looked like they had it all. Money clearly wasn't a problem for the family, and their grandfather's actions showed that cash didn't buy happiness. A man who pitted his sons against each other for his own sport couldn't have been the most fulfilled. Despite the facts, Eric's brothers seem to have turned out to be amazing people. And in this man's arms, she fell into a deep sleep.

By the time Romy woke, it was morning and she'd fallen so hard spittle crusted on the side of her mouth. When was the last time she slept that hard? She couldn't recall.

"Good morning." Eric's chest moved against her back as he spoke. The vibration sent warmth circling toward all her uniquely feminine places.

"How do you feel?" She separated herself from him slowly, so as not to accidentally cause him any pain.

"Like I lost the rodeo last night," he said with a chuckle. The chuckle turned into a cough.

She turned around in time to see him wince.

"I should take you back to the ranch this morning," she said. "There isn't much you can do in this state and it'll give you a few days to rest. I'll figure out a reason to stall or maybe we can release some false information to appease the jerk behind this. Buy more time."

"Have you heard from your sister?" he asked.

She gave a small headshake.

"Then, no. We're not leaving here without answers," he said. The determination in his voice left no room for doubt.

Would sneaking into Sasha's apartment reveal anything or were they on a wild goose chase?

12

"What are these?"

"I had clothes delivered." Eric had been up a solid two hours before the sun, rancher's blessing or curse depending on how he looked at it. He didn't normally flex his last name or bank account, but it didn't take much to get almost anything delivered in any amount of time these days.

"And I slept through it?" she asked with a shocked look.

He couldn't suppress his smile. "Sure did."

"How long have you been awake?" She rubbed her eyes.

"Long enough to pull up an app on my phone, and then have those show up," he said.

"Did you shower?" She seemed to size him up, still in disbelief he was capable of pulling off all those tasks.

"Guilty." He hadn't exactly pulled off a miracle. He'd been able to wash everything but his hair. Brushing his teeth had been the best part by far.

"And you're okay?" she asked.

"I had to rest after the shower, but I'll be fine," he said.

"I'm not easily broken and I'm already starting to feel better."

The way she looked at him said she doubted it. He needed to change the subject, then prove to her that it was worse than it looked. There wasn't much a good night of sleep couldn't cure, and he'd slept a little too well with Romy in his arms.

"Are you hungry? There's a room service menu on the desk." Just to prove he was doing better, he retrieved the menu and set it down on the bed next to her. Getting too close would be a bad idea when her hair was messy, her eyes sleepy, and her lips kissable.

She studied him for a long moment before picking up the menu. "I could pretty much eat anything on here."

"Coffee?" he asked, moving to the in-room machine.

"Yes, please."

"Cream? Sugar?" He picked up the box holding both and did his level best to stop his hand from shaking. The brain was interesting and didn't appreciate trauma. Duly noted.

"Black is the way I like it." She cocked her head to one side. "My birthday is October twenty-seventh."

The last comment came out of the blue.

"Okay." He drew out the *y*.

"I just thought you should know my birthday is two days before yours," she said.

"That makes us both October babies," he noted as the coffee machine, if he could call it that, spit and sputtered brown liquid into the paper cup. Once filled, he brought the first cup over to Romy before making his own. As if to prove he was doing fine despite standing, he moved over to the window to drink his instead of taking a seat. "Is there anything else I should know about you?"

Keeping his distance was near impossible when all he

wanted to do was return to bed with the beauty, but they weren't at the hotel for vacation.

"My favorite color is teal blue." She took a sip of fresh brew. "And, in general, I like a much stronger cup of coffee."

"Same here," he said after trying his.

"On the coffee or the color?" she asked. The genuine quality to her tone said she was curious.

"Coffee. All I have to do to see my favorite color is look in your eyes," he admitted.

"Oh."

"Anything else you want to know about me?" he asked, figuring he'd just overstepped his own boundary line.

There was a long pause. "I kind of want to know everything. Is that strange?"

"Not to me," he said. He had questions about her too.

"But I realize we're on a time crunch here, so I can hold off on other questions," she said.

"Ask me anything you want at any time. My life is an open book," he reassured. His answer seemed to satisfy her, but he couldn't figure out why the sudden need for knowledge. Unless she'd been more freaked out by the robbery than she let on. Or the very real fact their work together would finish soon, and she wanted to know as much as possible about him before it all came to a close. Another thought came to mind. Did she plan to carry on with the investigation by herself? Ditch him because she was worried about him getting hurt again?

"I plan to take you up on that," she said.

"Good. I plan to be around long enough to answer all your questions and more." His comment elicited a small smile. This seemed like a good time to steer the conversation back on track to the investigation. "I'm hoping we find something at your sister's place this morning. In case we don't, I have other plans in the works."

"Like?" she asked after taking another sip of coffee. She rolled the cup around in her hands, looking like she enjoyed the warmth.

"Since this whole mess is linked to my family, and I'm guessing the Marshall is at the heart of it, we might be able to dig around inside his business once we're back at home," he said.

"I'm not sure I should go back with you," she warned.

"Why is that?" he asked even though he was almost certain he knew the answer already.

"Look at what happened to you because of me," she stated. "I think it might be best if we split up. I can find a place to stay that won't bring these guys to your doorstep once we find my sister. I probably should have grabbed her and disappeared with her in the first place."

"And then what?" He had a feeling she'd gone into protective mode after what happened.

"I stay out of sight. So does my sister," she said.

"For how long?" he asked.

"However long it takes," she said with a shrug. Clearly, she hadn't done a whole lot of thinking. This was a knee-jerk reaction to last night's robbery.

"With your sister's condition, that might not be feasible. She may need to visit the doctor," he pointed out. "She might refuse to go into hiding with you. What did she say when she convinced you to spy on us?"

"That she wanted me to buy time for her," she said.

"For what?"

"So she could come up with a plan, I'm guessing. It all happened so fast. She didn't have much time and neither did I," she admitted.

"And now she'd gone missing—"

"Hold on a minute." She snapped her fingers together and sat up straighter. "I can't believe I didn't think about this before."

He took a sip of coffee and waited.

"I need my phone." She retrieved it from the counter and studied the screen as she thumbed her way onto the internet. The white bathrobe opened a little, revealing creamy skin. Not an image Eric needed in his mind while he was forcing himself to quash his attraction. He moved beside her and sat on the edge of bed so he could focus on her screen instead. The brilliant move only served to usher in her lavender scent.

She moved the phone out of his view.

"Doctor's orders," she said. "Remember? No screens."

Arguing wouldn't do any good based on the determined look on her face, even though he felt much better today. Plus, she was only trying to help. "Tell me what you're looking at."

"There was this spot she used to go to when we were kids. It's remote and I used to find her camping there when life got to be too much," she said. "What if she's there right now?"

"It's worth a shot."

"How much walking can you do?" she asked, biting her bottom lip.

"As much as I need to," he said.

"Be real with me, Eric," she insisted. "You're the toughest person I've ever met, but no going superhero on me and hurting your recovery in the process."

"Scout's honor," he promised.

"Well then, if that's the case, room service looks great and all, but it might be faster if we grab something to eat on the way out. Something we can take on the road with us," she said, studying him.

"Picking up food works for me." Eric hoped they would find answers at the mystery spot, because going to Sasha's apartment in broad daylight might fall into the category of too foolish to live.

THE FIRST GLIMMER of hope since this whole ordeal started lit a fire under Romy. She changed into the clean outfit from Eric—athletic shorts, sports top, and running shoes—before gathering her few belongings and heading out the door.

"Where are we headed?" Eric asked once they were inside his mother's Mercedes.

"McKinney Falls State Park," she supplied.

"If memory serves, that's south of here," he said. His mind was sharp and, based on the piece of paper she'd been given, that was a very good sign his head injury was recovering.

"That's right," she confirmed. "Cell coverage is spotty in certain areas and there's one place she might be."

It was a shot in the dark at best but there was no stone she'd leave unturned when it came to finding her sister. Sasha wouldn't likely be at her apartment anyway, so they would be going there for clues.

"There's a spot at Onion Creek where it spills over limestone edges and splashes into pools. It's hot outside so she loves to sit on the edge and stick her feet in the water," she said.

"When was the last time she was there?" he asked.

"It's been a few years as far as I know. But then, now that she's an adult, I don't exactly follow her around," she said.

He was right, though. This was probably a long shot. And yet, she couldn't let that stop her. If there was any chance her sister was there now or had been there at some point, Romy had to know.

"I know the area you're talking about," he said. "Popular spot."

"That's true. But she used to tell me if anything ever happened to her to go to a certain place there," she said, the memories flooding back. "Seems like she was always expecting to leave this earth young. I can't blame her with the childhood she had."

"A childhood made better by her older sister," he pointed out.

"It's so easy to blame myself for not getting there sooner. I keep thinking she might have turned out differently if I had. Don't get me wrong, I love my little sis, but she's always carried around an extra burden," she said.

"Without you, she probably wouldn't have survived this long," he said.

"Funny, I never really thought about it like that," she admitted.

"Don't sell yourself short," he said, his words a soothing balm to her soul.

"Thank you. I needed to hear something positive. When it comes to Sasha, it's so easy to fall into the trap of wishing I'd done better by her and blaming myself for not figuring it out sooner," she said.

"You weren't the only person in her life, and you were basically a kid. What you did was amazing, and someone should remind you of the fact every day."

Romy's eyes welled with tears. Before she could let those emotions take hold—emotions that threatened to pull her under and spin her out, she pulled into a popular coffee chain drive-thru and to the order window. She looked over at Eric. "What will you have?"

Between the two of them they ordered three breakfast sandwiches, two muffins, and twin coffees. Both were quiet while paying and pulling back onto the highway. Eric situated their meal in between them.

"I'm not hungry yet. Go ahead and eat without me. I'll just sip on this coffee until we get there," she said.

"Are you sure?" he asked.

"I don't want to waste any more time getting to the park." She wished she could reel those words in the minute they left her mouth. "I didn't mean that you caused me to waste time—"

"Don't worry about it. We're both frustrated by the setback from the robbery," he said, calm as anyone pleased.

When she put her foot in her mouth, he seemed to realize what she meant instead of what she said. Eric offered the kind of encouragement she needed more than anything when she was at her worst. He soothed her when she blamed herself. The man was a keeper for someone. If they'd met under different circumstances, she could see the possibility of that person being her. Plus, despite their mutual attraction and incredible chemistry, what did she really know about him? Didn't fires that burned the brightest burn out the fastest? How many relationships had she seen her sister in that started off with a bang and ended up fizzling out? More than Romy wanted to count.

A voice in the back of her mind pointed out she would have found a reason to mess up a relationship with Eric or walk away. Romy didn't do long-term with anyone, no matter how strong the physical attraction might be. After hearing herself talk about her emotionally-distant mother, a father who loved her but was incapable of taking care of her when she was young, and a half-sister who desperately needed help, it was no wonder Romy kept most people at arm's length. Had there ever been someone in her life she could trust? *Really trust?* Romy realized she didn't do trust with anyone. Could she with Eric? Her heart wanted to more than anything. But...

And there would always be a *but*. She feared it would only be a matter of time before one of them walked. A person like Eric could truly shatter her. Could she risk it?

The funny thing was that a relationship wasn't even on the table at this point. Despite feeling more chemistry with Eric than she'd experienced with anyone her entire life, the two of them weren't dating. In fact, her brain picked that moment to remind her they wouldn't even know each other at all if she hadn't been sent to spy on his family's business. How was that for a story to tell their children? Grandchildren?

Romy was beginning to think she'd been the one to take a blow to the head. She never really saw herself as having a family. Her businesses were going to be her 'babies' and she was fine with that. Her hands were full with Sasha. Now that her sister was going to have a baby, Romy would need to step up and help them both. She couldn't stand the thought of another child being left to their own defenses and didn't think Sasha was ready for the responsibility.

And yet, knowing all this, why was she suddenly thinking about a small house on ranch property with Eric, and a couple of kids running around?

13

The drive to the park was quiet after the quick food stop. Romy insisted on driving as Eric leaned the seat back and rested his eyes. The only way she felt comfortable leaving the hotel was if he rested as much as possible.

Before she knew it, she was exiting McKinney Falls Parkway. She drove around the Big Oak Camping Area before parking near the Upper Falls. The fact Sasha hadn't responded to any of Romy's texts continued to weigh heavily on her thoughts. Normally, she would chalk it up to her sister in one of her moods. This was different. Sasha was in trouble.

This seemed like a good time to remind herself of the fact no one would hurt Sasha until Romy gave them what they wanted. Speaking of which, she was supposed to hand over something by now. Everything was happening so fast, she hadn't thought about checking in. No one had contacted her.

Romy put the gearshift in park and cut off the engine.

Eric sat straight up and shook his head like he was trying to shake fog out of his brain.

"Everything okay?" she asked, studying him, needing to know he wasn't pushing himself too far for her.

"As long as I keep these on." He picked up the Ray-Bans and slid them over the bridge of his nose. Her stomach free fell when he turned to her. His hooded gaze gave him an even sexier edge.

"Good," she said, and she could hear the crick in her own throat.

Rather than draw attention to her embarrassment, she exited the vehicle and met him around the front. Eric was quick to move, a huge improvement over the last few hours.

"That was fast thinking last night, by the way," he said. "Going for my ankle holster."

"I took a risk I maybe shouldn't have taken," she said. "It could have gone really wrong."

"But it didn't, and your instincts are solid," he said. "You might have saved both of our lives if the men were involved in this mess, rather than just being robbers."

She nodded.

"You are a capable person, Romy. Do you realize that?" One of his eyebrows shot up above the sunglasses. "Do you know how much more beautiful that makes you?"

She cleared her throat.

"Thank you, Eric."

Romy had always been a roll-her-sleeves-up type and was beginning to notice how uncomfortable compliments made her feel. Why was that?

In her mind, there was always something more to be done, so there was no time to stand around and congratulate herself on all her accomplishments. He had a point, though. It was good to stop every once in a while and take stock. There was a time before she started her business when the bakery was all she could think about. All her hopes, prayers, and dreams were rolled into building a successful venture from the ground up. Since she loved baking, it seemed like the most natural choice.

Eric reached for her hand, linking their fingers. The connection both excited and calmed her.

"The spot my sister used to love to come to isn't too far from here," she said, getting her thoughts back on track to why they were there in the first place.

"This would be so much easier if we could just investigate it properly. Go to her job and ask who'd been picking her up from work," Eric stated.

"It's hard when everything has to be done under the radar," she admitted.

"What about friends?" he continued.

"My sister had friends in the moment, like she would talk to people at work but when she needed a shoulder to cry on that was usually me," Romy said. Her sister was a floater in life and Romy figured half the reason Sasha never let anyone get close to her was because of the trauma she'd experienced as a child. "I doubt she had any long-term friendships, but I haven't exactly stalked her social media accounts. She doesn't really post very often anyway and I'm rarely ever on my personal account. I only got online for my bakery anyway. Personally, I prefer to live my life without a camera or a screen. I like to be active and I'm basically a private person."

"Couldn't have said it better myself," Eric agreed. "Having a website is good for the ranch. That's about as far as it goes for me, but then I've never been one to have an electronic device glued to my hand. It just never appealed."

"Comes in handy for business," she agreed, thinking the

two of them had more in common than she wanted to notice or admit. Although, she did want to lean into his strength, if only for a little while.

Romy walked to the upper falls as beads of sweat trickled down her face. The heat slammed her square in the face; no matter how long she lived in Texas, she would never get used to the punishing sun in August.

From the path, she could hear the splashes of folks jumping into the natural pools below the falls. Voices carried, laughter. Even though Romy knew it was impossible for her sister to be here, she listened for the sounds of her voice anyway.

Her pulse kicked up a few notches as she realized how exposed they were. She tightened her grip on his fingers. He brought her hand to his lips and pressed a tender kiss on the back of hers.

"We're okay," he soothed. The fact he appeared so calm should comfort her. Nothing about being outside after what happened last night made her relax.

She searched every face as she walked past, thinking how close they'd come to dying.

Romy shook it off. She couldn't get inside her head about what might have been. All she could do was focus on the here and now. Remind herself they were fine when panic tried to take over. Because they *were* fine. They were better than fine.

A new resolve kicked in, giving Romy the boost of confidence she needed. Only Sasha had this effect on Romy.

Walking through the tree line near the falls, she scanned the ground, looking for a clue her sister had been here. Just when she thought this whole idea was a waste of time, she saw material peeking out from a stack of rocks. The pink and white checker pattern spiked Romy's pulse. "There's something over here."

She moved to the stack of rocks and pulled out her sister's favorite ragdoll. Miss Penelope was covered in dirt. Tears welled as Romy dusted the doll off.

"What's this?" Eric asked.

"This is Miss Penelope. My sister used to send me notes through this doll," Romy said, turning Miss Penelope over. She unsnapped the back of her dress where there was Velcro on the doll's back, suppressing the hope there would be a note inside telling Romy all of this had been an elaborate hoax. Part of her wished this could be solved that simply so she could apologize to Eric and move on with her life. Even before the emergency call had come from her sister, Romy had felt stuck. Stuck in life. Stuck in relationships. Stuck in work.

Shoving those thoughts aside for now, she pushed her fingers through the Velcro. Sure enough, there was a piece of paper tucked inside. Romy glanced up at Eric, locking gazes for a few seconds before retrieving the folded up piece of paper.

Her fingers couldn't open the slip fast enough. There was a name that had been hastily scribbled. *Randol Kinkaid.*

"You do know who that is, don't you?" Eric asked.

"Isn't he in politics?" she asked.

"He's one of the most influential men in Texas who doesn't have the last name Firebrand," Eric stated plainly. "He's almost constantly at the governor's side."

"Right. Now, I know who you're talking about." She snapped her fingers. "He's a lawyer."

"And he owns a private equity firm," Eric said. "He tried to get my family in on an investment deal to develop land outside of Austin but it encroached on a park. The Marshall said they'd never get the right permits to build. This guy says he can get it done anyway. We walked away from the deal. There was one thing the Marshall purely loved, and that was Texas. He groaned about the offer for a while and then it died on the vine."

"And now you said someone's been trying to buy up land around the ranch, plus interfere with Firebrand business," she pointed out.

"That's right. I didn't think about Kinkaid because the deal fell through last year. The only reason I know about it at all is because he came to me when the Marshall refused to do business," Eric said. "Asked if I would speak to my grandfather."

"What did you say?" She couldn't imagine that went over well.

"If he didn't get anywhere with my grandfather, then me talking to him wouldn't change the answer," he said on a chuckle. "Clearly, the man had no idea who or what he was dealing with. No one overrode the Marshall."

More of those puzzle pieces clicked together. "I have one question. Is this man blackmailing my sister, or is he the father of her child?"

"He claims to be a family man. It's the platform he does business on," Eric stated. "Yank that out from underneath him and he'll lose a lot of investors."

The name inside the doll made Romy believe Randol Kinkaid was the father of Sasha's child. *Oh, Sasha. What a mess.*

"After I spoke to Randol Kinkaid, I did a little digging into his background. The conversation had me wondering if I was making a mistake by not pushing the issue with the Marshall." Eric hoped the baby didn't belong to Kinkaid. The man was lower than dirt when it came to morals.

"And?"

"I have a file back at home in the Marshall's office. We can take a look at it together when we return to the ranch. There are quite a few details in there. On the high level, he's not the kind of guy you want your sister around." He hated to be the bearer of bad news. "There were several mistresses in his background. He also has a wife and four kids under the age of twelve."

Romy gasped. "What a jerk."

"You can say that again," he said. "Beyond that, he had a string of unhappy business partners, failed business ventures. There were successes too and I figured his friendship with the governor helped a whole lot with that."

"What has my sister gotten herself into?" she asked low and under her breath.

He reached out to touch her arm, offering reassurance. She surprised him by leaning into him.

"Underneath it all, there's a lot of good inside her," she said on a sigh. "It probably doesn't look like it on the surface, but she is truly a kind person. I've never seen her swat at a fly. She just opened a window or door and scooted them on their way."

"A guy like Kinkaid can be charismatic when he wants something. He had me checking into his background to see if I'd made a mistake by not supporting him," Eric said. Knowing who was involved complicated the situation. His hope that this whole ordeal could be dealt with and over quickly died on the vine. If Kinkaid was the father of Sasha's baby, he would be in her life for a long time to come, and the threat to Romy's sister would never let up because she would have too much power over Kinkaid. He wouldn't want to have a bastard child linked to him. The question was how far would Kinkaid go to keep the news quiet?

"My sister can be naïve despite a harsh upbringing. She's smart but not savvy if that makes any sense. She can be manipulated," Romy continued.

Eric glanced around, thinking how exposed they were out in the open like this. This was clearly Sasha's safe hiding spot based on the finding, but how long would it last? They were lucky to have found the doll first, in his opinion.

"How about we get out of here?" he asked Romy. They had a lot to digest with this new information.

"Good idea," she said, taking in a deep breath. She tucked the piece of paper back inside the doll, and the doll under her arm. "Miss Penelope is going with us."

"The doll is the only proof we have right now of Kinkaid's involvement," he said.

"So I'm not risking anything happening to her by leaving her here unattended where a kid could find her or worse," she pointed out.

He nodded, thinking it was best to keep Sasha's insurance policy with the two of them. Before they left, he slipped his phone out of his pocket and snapped a couple of pics of the spot where Romy had found the doll. More evidence.

"Do you think it's still a good idea to go to my sister's apartment?" Romy asked.

"It's a terrible idea," he quickly countered. "But we have to do it in case she's there and needs our help."

"What are you thinking? Saunter on in during the day?" she asked as they made their way back to his mother's Mercedes.

"We need a cover. We can check out one of those meal delivery services and maybe grab a magnet off someone's vehicle in front of a restaurant," he said. "It would be best if only one of us was visible but it's easy enough to keep someone tucked in the backseat out of view."

"The ballcap should help disguise you and since they could be expecting me it might be best if you're the one who goes up to her door," she said. "I have a key, so all you have to do is knock and then slip inside. I can even keep watch from across the lot in between cars to make sure no one follows you."

By the time they made it back to the Mercedes, they had a solid plan in place. Risky but solid.

He checked the clock on the dashboard. "It's close to lunch. We could slip in under the guise of a lunch delivery."

"Anyone who knows my sister would realize she loves Torchy Tacos," she supplied.

"Torchy's it is," he agreed. "The last time I was in Austin, I noticed the delivery driver's had magnets on their doors. It should be easy enough to grab one if we're patient."

Eric sat in the parking lot of one of the most popular take-out places in Austin according to its rating on the app called Take Out. It was a Tex-Mex place called MexiTex. Easy enough to find. Easy enough to stalk a driver considering the first five parking spots closest to the door were marked To-Go Only.

Eric didn't have to wait long for a delivery driver to show. He took down the guy's license plate so he could reimburse him for the sign once this was said and done. He would do it now if not for the fact all cash had been stolen last night. His head was still sore but improving, and his ego was a whole lot bruised for letting those guys get the jump on him. Right now, he classified the whole incident as water under the bridge and lesson learned. He wouldn't make the mistake of parking on a seedy street in the pitch black and then stopping to make out. The move had been beyond stupid on his part. He knew better. He got a little too comfortable with Romy and a little too overconfident in himself. The headache reminded him that he wasn't invincible.

Plus, he couldn't regret the progress they'd made. They had a name. Randol Kinkaid. He might lead them to answers. But first, they were ready to go to Sasha's apartment to see what they could find there.

14

Eric reluctantly let Romy drive. His hesitation had nothing to do with being macho and everything to do with the fact someone could end up following them. He chased and had been chased by poachers on the ranch, so he had experience in evasion. She did not. His stance was purely practical.

After glancing at the piece of paper the nurse had given her with release instructions, letting her drive was the only choice. Under no circumstances was he to use a screen and he was supposed to minimize exposure to sunlight. The Ray-Bans were doing their job, blocking out a good portion of the sun. On the passenger side, he could use his forearm to shade himself further.

If he was driving and had to accelerate, the images would come at him too fast and could trigger a worse headache. Hard to imagine that was even possible. At times, his vision blurred as it was. He couldn't afford that to happen in the case of a highspeed chase. It was one thing to put his own life at risk, an entirely other to be responsible for another human being.

There was a bonus to riding shotgun. Giving up the driver's seat meant he could scan the area and watch out for suspicious persons. Austin had a definite vibe, even this time of year. The sidewalks were still crowded, and the roads always had traffic no matter the time of day, save for the sideroads like the one they'd been on last night.

There was something niggling at the back of his mind about Randol Kinkaid, something Eric couldn't pinpoint. Whatever it was, he felt certain he'd be able to find it in the file back home.

His cell buzzed and Romy put up a finger that practically dared him to pick it up.

"I'll pull over at the next parking lot," she said with a stern look that would make any teenager shake in their boots.

He cracked a smile.

Romy put on her blinker and he watched through the side view mirror to see if anyone dared to follow them. This was probably a good test to see if they'd picked up a tail of any kind. No one followed or seemed interested in where they went.

As soon as Romy pulled into a spot in the fast-food chain parking lot, he handed over his cell. She took the offering and checked the screen. "It's a text from your mother."

"What does it say?" For a split-second, his heart sank. The thought his father's condition had somehow worsened brought on a wave of unexpected sadness.

"Your dad is improving and your mother wanted everyone to know that he's sitting up, asking about his children," she said.

Those words were some of the most shocking he'd heard. Brodie Firebrand wanted to know how his children were doing? Did Eric have residual anger toward his father for not having anything to do with them growing up? Yes. The family secrets that were coming out made his hands fist. But there was something about the idea of never having the chance to make it right, like with the Marshall, that had been sitting heavy on Eric's chest.

Did that magically mean everything was forgiven? No. Not even close. It just meant there was a possibility for healing he didn't want permanently erased. His father had a big hill to climb when it came to making amends for the past. He couldn't do that if he died.

"Better late than never," he mumbled before adding, "did she say anything else?"

"Just that she didn't want anyone to worry. His condition is looking up and the two of them are doing a lot of talking," she said.

"Is that in the family group chat?" he asked.

"Looks like it. Yes," she informed.

"Has anyone else responded?" he asked.

"Doesn't look like it," she said.

Very soon, they needed to have a family meeting without their parents. Clear the air. See where everyone stood. A couple of his brothers had far deeper wounds to heal with their father and Eric wanted them to have first dibs. His biggest complaint was having no relationship with the man. Brothers like Brax and Dane had deeper scars.

"Do you want to talk about it?" She reached over and touched his hand. There was something healing about their connection. Two broken souls finding comfort with each other? Could there be more between them than fire and off-the-charts chemistry? Because he'd never felt so connected to someone he barely knew before, not even Lynn. This was new territory and he had no idea where it would lead. Would it burn out or could it be the real deal?

Right now, someone else was on Eric's mind. Kinkaid.

"No. Not really," he admitted, circling back to Romy's question after a few beats of silence sat between them. "But if I did, it would be with you."

Her small smile was all the reward he needed.

"Right now, all I want to think about is Kinkaid. We need to figure out the connection to your sister since we already know what he's after with the ranch. He's taking a potshot now that the Marshal is gone. Kinkaid figures we're weak with my father in the hospital and all the arguing going on at the ranch. None of it can be a secret with all the press we've been getting lately."

No one had to be plugged in to realize the Marshal's sons would be at each other's throats. It was common knowledge. He wondered if Uncle Kief had even bothered to visit his brother while he was in the hospital. It wouldn't come as a shock to learn he hadn't.

"Promise to talk to me once we're square with my sister?" Romy asked. The question hinted at a future beyond this case and was surprisingly welcome. She'd somehow tunneled her way into his heart and no matter what else happened between them, he would always have a soft spot for her. Once in, always in. He could say that with confidence because no one had made him feel the same in all his years of dating.

"Deal," he said firmly.

His answer seemed to satisfy her because she backed out of the parking spot and then navigated back onto the road they'd been on before the interruption.

With some effort, Eric put the text message out of his mind because he could go into a real tailspin trying to figure out how this might change all of their relationships. Eric couldn't help but wonder about his brothers who'd immediately left the ranch, like his brother Fallon. He'd joined the military and rarely made contact. Had there been a trauma like Dane's that caused their younger brother to ditch town and not look back?

Dane had been taken on a poaching trip with their father when he'd caught the man in an affair in the tent beside his. He'd shot what he believed had been a wild animal, run away, and then had been sworn to secrecy about the affair by their father and the Marshal. *Great parenting.*

Rather than break an oath, Dane bolted after graduating high school and rarely looked back. Now that Eric knew the circumstances, he could wring his father's neck. Of course, thoughts like that brought on a wave of guilt after the man's heart attack. And yet, Eric had no idea what to do with all this pent-up anger. Normally, he'd work out hard to release some of the tension. His mind could think up another way to burn off his frustration. It involved burying himself inside Romy and getting lost long enough to forget how messed up his family could truly be. But when he made love to her, he wanted it to mean more than an escape, no matter how tempting that might be.

Eric stopped himself right there. In his mind, he already had the two of them making love. When did that shift take place? Last he remembered, he was figuring out ways to keep a distance from the heat sizzling between them. His raging headache was a good reminder of what could happen if he lost focus. He didn't even want to think about what might have happened if those two men had been Kinkaid's guys. And there was no way Kinkaid would do his own dirty work. He would hire out to bring in someone more qualified to get the job done neat and clean. He would also keep as much of a distance as possible from the actual crimes. Leaving a trail like that one would end his marriage, his career, and his standing in the community. Randol Kinkaid couldn't allow that to happen.

The man was a real piece of work. Not as stupid as Eric had first believed, so he wouldn't underestimate the guy again. It had been easy to dig up dirt on him. Easy for Eric and his investigator. But then Eric only hired the best. He had to keep a low profile too and there were certain affairs involving the family business that needed to stay under the radar.

The smallest piece of information turned into click-bait, which in turn damaged the family's reputation whether the tidbit was true or not. Folks didn't read much past the headlines.

"We're two blocks away and that means you're going to have to take the driver's seat from here," Romy said as she pulled off the road into another parking lot. It was full so she just pulled behind a couple of cars and left the engine idling as they switched seats.

The way she looked at him when they crossed paths said she was worried about this change.

"I'll be okay for the short drive. The speed limit is low here. I've been watching to see if anyone is following us, which is hard to do in this traffic anyway," he said, hoping to ease some of the tension lines in her forehead.

"We're close. I think you'll be okay. I'm worried about what you might find inside my sister's apartment." She'd slipped into the backseat, reaching for the ragdoll that had been tucked away there. She held it pressed to her chest, he figured, for moral support as she got low and stayed there.

"We'll deal with it together," he promised, liking the sound of those words as he heard them come out of his own mouth. He'd always operated alone and preferred it that way. Something inside him was shifting, changing. He was thinking in terms of 'us' and 'we.'

There was no reason to fight what would never materialize into anything anyway. How could it? This wasn't the time to worry about it either. Yes, something special was happening between them. No, he couldn't stop thinking about her. But he needed to, and he needed to do it ASAP or risk another head injury. Or worse.

As he neared the apartment, he skimmed the faces of the college kids as they walked by, backpacks slung over one shoulder. They looked hot, of the pavement melting variety. Eric was used to the soaring summer temperatures despite doing much of his work indoors. There was always something he needed to do to pitch in with manual labor on a cattle ranch. He rode his horse, Castle, nearly every morning to get the day going.

Pulling into the lot, he grabbed the ballcap and lowered it so the rim hit the top of his Ray-Bans. His t-shirt and jeans wouldn't draw attention. His boots might. Then again, Austin had just about every type of person under the sun. Variety was part of the city's appeal.

"I need something in my hands." He glanced around. Romy handed over the fast food bag from breakfast. It would do in a pinch and this definitely qualified. She also put the apartment key in the palm of his hand.

He pulled into a visitor spot near the building and left the car running as he dashed upstairs. The door was ajar and that most definitely wasn't a good sign. It probably meant the coast was clear for Romy to come upstairs but he didn't want to risk it in case someone was watching the place. He doubted even a man like Kinkaid would have enough resources to cover this apartment, Sasha, and keep tabs on the ranch. It was a lot of ground to cover and seemed unlikely. Still, he wouldn't take anything for granted. Not this time.

Eric knocked on the door, mostly for show in the event someone was out there. He slipped inside as a musty smell assaulted him. He'd been around dead animals before, so he was familiar with the odor. Thankfully, that wasn't what he smelled here. This place had the day-old, spoiled food left out on the counter smell.

Using his shoulder, he eased his way inside. The minute he was safely out of view from eyes outside, he set down the bag and scanned the room. It could best be described as signs of a struggle present. A lamp was knocked over next to the sofa. The room itself had an eclectic vibe. Beads over the hallway. Feathers on lampshades. The sofa looked like it had maybe been donated and she'd put a slipcover over it. Throw pillows were scattered on the beige carpet. A glass had been knocked over and the contents spilled.

The kitchen was too small for a table but a counter-height bar that separated it from the living room had a pair of barstools for seating. He slipped through the beads, checking the bedroom and its closet before clearing the master bath. Eric moved through the space, ensuring it was clear. The apartment itself consisted of three rooms and a bathroom. Based on the open cabinet doors and the suitcase that had been flung on the floor, it looked like Sasha was trying to get out when she was interrupted.

This wasn't the news Eric wanted to bring back to Romy, especially considering her sister had gone dark within hours of contacting her to become a spy. He double-checked every nook and cranny of the apartment, not wanting to leave any stone unturned.

On the way out, he checked the stack of bills on the

counter in between the kitchen and living room. He wasn't certain what he was looking for. Any correspondence. Although, he couldn't remember the last time he sent a letter. All business was conducted over e-mail and text. Even confirmation of his hay orders came in via text. But wouldn't there be some evidence of a romantic link between her and Kinkaid or whoever the father might be?

Sadly, all the evidence would most likely be on her cell phone. Even if the father wasn't Kinkaid, both would go to great lengths to keep the affair a secret. There were no cards in sight. It was summer, not exactly a romantic holiday like Valentine's Day, so he shouldn't be too surprised there. If only they had access to Sasha's cell phone. There had to be evidence on it. Texts. Meet ups.

Other than the apartment door being broken into, this trip was a bust. He didn't look forward to delivering this news to Romy and he needed to get back to the Mercedes where she waited hunkered down in the backseat. The thought anything could happen to her sent a lead fireball to the pit of his stomach.

A thought struck. Could he bring his brothers into the fight? They deserved to know someone was coming after the ranch. They would also rally around Romy.

He dismissed the idea. Everyone had enough on their plates with the death of their grandfather and the hospitalization of their father. He didn't want to add to the burden. Then again, they might be offended if he didn't allow them a chance to help. Eric and Romy needed to have a conversation about next steps.

As he walked toward the door, he caught a glimpse of white in the sofa underneath the cushion. Eric crossed the room. There was a sharp corner sticking out. A card? He grabbed it and opened it. Sure enough, there was a picture of a bouquet of flowers on the front. This screamed romance. He opened the card and read the private note.

Sasha,

This child is a blessing. In time, you'll see. Know that I love you and can't wait to bring our baby into this world. Until I leave my wife, secrecy is the only way. Be strong, my angel.

Love,

RK

THIS HAD to be from Randol Kinkaid based on the initials. Between this card and the ragdoll, there was sufficient proof Sasha's baby belonged to him. And, yes, the scandal would rock the man's world.

Eric couldn't get out of there fast enough. He closed the door, despite the lock being jammed, and got to the Mercedes as fast as he possible. A tsunami of relief washed over him when he saw Romy there hunkered down in the backseat. He couldn't wait to tell her what he'd found even though part of the news would shake her to the core.

"Did you get anything?" she immediately asked as she claimed the driver's seat. The sun felt like it might burn holes through his eyes but he kept the sunglasses on and his hat low.

"Yes," was all he said before she put the gearshift in reverse and backed out of the lot.

Within a few minutes, she was able to pull over into a parking lot and stop for a moment. After she parked, the two of them stepped outside, and then ditched the magnet for the delivery service. This wasn't news she should see or hear while driving.

He produced the card and waited for her to react while

she read it. Rather than have a complete meltdown, she locked onto his gaze.

"This confirms what we feared most. Randol Kinkaid is the father of my sister's child," she said, those blue eyes clear and intent.

"I believe so," he agreed.

"What about her apartment?" she asked.

He described the condition and where he found the card.

"That's not a good sign, Eric." She stepped closer to him, leaning into him.

This time, he scanned the area, determined not to be a victim twice. Still, he couldn't stop himself from wrapping his arms around her. He liked the feel of her against his chest. The way her breathing fell into a perfect rhythm with his. And he especially liked the way she looked up at him with a gaze that bordered on need.

"We'll find her." It was the best reassurance he could offer and yet fell short in every sense. It was a promise he wanted to keep even though he had no idea if that was even possible. A visit to Randol Kinkaid might provide answers.

15

"We need to find him."

Romy balked at the suggestion. It seemed like the surest way to get her sister killed. "Randol Kinkaid?"

"It's the fastest way to get to your sister." Eric nodded.

"Maybe. But it doesn't seem like the safest option." She couldn't imagine that showing their hand would be the right play, but she was willing to listen to Eric's reasoning.

"Blackmail can work both ways," he said. "I had Kinkaid investigated when he proposed to do business with my family. I have a file on him back at the ranch. All I have to do is give him a call and tell him we make an exchange or I go to the feds."

A whoosh sounded in Romy's ears as her pulse kicked up a few notches. This felt a whole lot like playing chicken with her sister's life. "It's dangerous."

"We're short on options," he pointed out.

"That's true. And my sister is in trouble," she said.

"Time could be the enemy," he added.

"I need a minute to think this through," she said.

Jumping before examining all the angles was a risk she wouldn't normally take.

"We can keep talking it through if you want," he said.

"I hear what you're saying, but I'm afraid to poke the bear," she said.

"It's sometimes the only way to know if the bear is bluffing. Look, Kinkaid is involved. That much we know for certain," he said.

"Right," she confirmed.

"And your sister might be in serious danger," he continued.

"That's true." Her brain was trying to process.

"I'd be the last person who would want to make a call that causes any harm to your sister or you," he said and the anguished look in his eyes said he meant it.

She compressed her lips into a frown and nodded.

"Right now, we're playing defense. Before, we didn't even know who our opponent was," he said.

"We do now," she said.

"Exactly. Kinkaid is the father. The likelihood those were someone else's initials on the card is as close to zero as we'll get. He'll know we can check the handwriting with an expert, and he can't take the bad publicity. His family will most likely turn on him. His businesses will fail when partners bolt. Not even the governor himself will be able to save his buddy no matter how close the two of them are. Governors are politicians and they have to distance themselves from drama," Eric said. "Much of Kinkaid's business rests on his fabricated reputation. Not many families are formidable enough to go after him while he is so close to the governor. Firebrands are one of the few who have the kind of power to challenge him. We can do some serious damage and I'll make sure he knows it."

He was right on every count. And yet, this was Sasha they were talking about. Her life might hang in the balance and their next moves could be damaging if not deadly to a sister Romy was born to protect.

"What if by some strange coincidence he isn't the father?" she asked.

"It's safe to say he's involved. He'll know we aren't playing around." Eric put his hands on her shoulders. The move grounded and comforted her. "We have something that will cause Kincaid to shake in his boots...proof. The other thing we have going for us is my family name. There's a reason he's not coming directly at us. We're powerful. Our name opens doors and, in his case, jail cells."

"Let's talk through how all this might go down," she said, noticing how much more he squinted against the bright sunlight even with glasses on. She needed to get him inside somewhere. "But not here."

"We need a safe place to work from," he said. "And if I'm honest, I need to sit down."

It looked like it pained him to admit he needed a break.

"Let's get back inside your mom's car and I'll look up a hotel," she said.

"We never officially checked out of the last one. Maybe we could just extend our stay another day or so," he said.

She had hoped that all this would be behind them before the sun went down. The possibility of seeing her sister again, safe and alive, strengthened her resolve.

As much as she wanted this nightmare to be over, she also wasn't quite ready to go back to her life before Eric. Could she have both?

∼

Despite a raging headache, a plan was taking shape. Eric figured it was safe to pop a couple of ibuprofens at this point and hoped the pills could keep the mind-numbing pain from getting worse. Food would help. The small breakfast they'd had wasn't nearly enough to keep his stomach from rumbling.

At this level of weakness, he couldn't afford a physical confrontation. Even someone with half his strength would have a shot to take him down at this point. Adrenaline could only get him so far and his body was already telling him to slow down and rest.

"Do you want to stop off for food and supplies, or go straight to the hotel?" Romy asked, taking the driver's seat.

"I need food pretty quick and something for pain," he said. "Caffeine would be a bonus."

He hadn't wanted to risk making his headache worse earlier so despite making a cup at the hotel this morning and the coffee they'd gotten with breakfast sandwiches he'd only taken a few sips. The lack of caffeine was starting to show.

Romy worked on her phone for a few minutes while he fumbled around for the chair release lever. Found it. A few seconds later, his seat was in a reclined position. He closed his eyes. The current pain level caused his stomach to roil.

"Got it. We're all set," Romy said before starting the vehicle and getting back on the road.

Many of Austin's downtown streets were in need of repair. Every bump caused a painful echo inside his skull, making it next to impossible to think clearly. He needed to pull up his bootstraps and rally. There was no way he intended to let Romy down this close to the finish line.

It didn't take long for her to pull off the road again. He blinked his eyes open, wincing against the bright light.

"Where are we?" he asked, figuring it was easier to ask than try to get his bearings by looking around.

She named a familiar fast food BBQ chain. He ordered the rib meal with extra sides. It was probably a good sign overall for his health that his appetite was back.

Within ten minutes, the two of them were back at the hotel with food and ibuprofen in hand. The meal tasted better than it probably was. Eating while starving always improved the flavor.

"Give me ten minutes to close my eyes. Then, coffee," he requested. Then, he remembered the file at home. "Hold on. Grab my phone and pretend to be me on a text message. Ask for one of my brothers, whoever is in the house, to go into the Marshal's files and locate the one marked with Randol Kinkaid's name. I can't give them an exact location, but my best guess is that the Marshal kept it in his desk file."

He heard shuffling noises and then it went quiet. By the time he woke, two hours had passed.

"Sorry about crashing on you," he said, sitting up and rubbing blurry eyes.

"Don't worry about it." She waved him off like it was nothing, but the stress cracks around her eyes told a different story. "And try not to move too quickly."

Trying to move much more would be a problem before he was fully awake.

"Hold on a sec." She made a cup of coffee and surprised him by handing it over instead of drinking it herself.

"Thank you for this," he said as she scooted over beside him. She sat so close he could breathe in her clean, lavender scent. Their outer thighs touched and the familiar electric current coursed through him.

"You're welcome," she said, slowing lifting his left arm as she positioned herself in the nook. "Is that okay?"

"You won't hear any complaining on my end." In fact, he was about to make the move himself. He hadn't wanted to surprise her or cross any boundaries despite the strong sexual current running between them. "Plus, I can't stop thinking about you."

He'd said the last bit low and under his breath. It didn't matter if she heard him or not because he needed to say the words out loud for his own benefit. His heart defied logic, falling for a woman he might not be able to hold onto. Logic said they barely knew each other despite his heart arguing the opposite. Granted, he might not know every detail of her life before they met, but deep down where it counted, he felt like he'd known her all his life.

But how long before she was ready to move on from Lone Star Pass? Before she was ready to start a new business? Once she got her sister back, reason said she would move back to Austin to be nearby in order to support the pregnancy then help with the baby.

If their mission didn't go as planned, would she ever be able to look at him or be at the ranch again? Would she see him as the person who'd caused her sister to go away permanently?

The thought struck a dark chord. Considering anything but bringing Sasha home was off the table. He would only consider a successful outcome, even though he would run all scenarios in his mind in order to be prepared for anything. In his experience with poachers, *anything* happened. In this case, they were dealing with an investor, a man linked to a governor.

"Have we heard back from my family?" he asked.

"Adam had an auto-response warning that he might be out of cell phone range. Corbin responded, saying he was on his way back to the main house but that it might take a minute for him to get there. Said he'd be in touch as soon as he got to the office. It's the reason I didn't disturb you while you slept. That, and the obvious reason you needed to get rest."

She blinked up at him and more of those campfires lit inside his chest.

"I'm doing better," he said, trying to ease some of the worry lines etched in her forehead.

"I can't think of anything bad happening to you, Eric," she said and her voice cracked with emotion.

"It won't." They both knew he might not be able to keep that promise. This wasn't the time for reality. This was the time for reassurance. With that, he dipped his head and kissed her. She tasted like dark roast coffee and honey. Her lavender scent washed over him as he took in a breath and all he could think was more. He wanted more of her. More of her skin pressed to his. More of her soft lips against his. More of her beside him, under him, and on top of him.

His cell buzzed, cutting into the moment, which was probably a good thing in the long run. It was a little too easy to get lost with Romy and they didn't have a whole lot of time to burn.

Romy checked the screen. "It's your brother Corbin saying he's at the main house."

"Would you mind calling him on speaker?" he asked.

"Not a bit."

She did and within a few seconds, his brother's voice was on the line.

"Hey, what's so important?" Corbin asked.

"I'm with our new office assistant and the call is on speaker," Eric informed.

"Sounds good." Corbin was unfazed.

"Like I mentioned, there's a file probably in the

Marshal's desk marked with the name *Randol Kinkaid*. I need the contents read to me," Eric stated. "Fair warning, I had him investigated when he wanted to do business with the Marshal."

"Okay." Corbin gave them the minute-by-minute as he entered the office area. Sounds of him unlocking the drawer and sifting through files came across the line as he whistled. There'd always been something right about working with his brothers despite the recent drama and crimes that seemed to follow them. No matter what else happened, they could always count on each other.

He thought about Romy and wondered who ever had her back. Who did she have to work with other than people who were paid to be there? It wasn't the same as having family who would do anything for one another.

As much as she loved her sister, the basis of their relationship put Romy as the caregiver. There didn't seem to be anything mutual about it except maybe she slept better at night knowing her sister was safe. There was a lot to be said for peace of mind. He wouldn't discount its benefits. And yet, he also wanted more for her.

"I'm not seeing anything here," Corbin reported.

"Did you check the very back?" It was possible the Marshal kept the file as hidden as possible.

"Any chance he digitized it?" Corbin asked.

"None." Eric almost laughed out loud at the thought the Marshal would even think to do such a thing. He had a computer in his office that mostly collected dust. "This isn't the kind of file he would want a hacker to be able to access, if you know what I mean."

"Oh. Well then. I walked in on him once when he was digging out a piece of paper from a compartment under his desk. Maybe..." A few seconds passed before Corbin let out a victory whoop. "Found it. And you're right about our grandfather not being too fond of keeping anything important on the computer. I remember how long it took you to convince him to let you use the computer for accounting."

"The man could be an ox," Eric confirmed with a smile. The Marshal had good qualities. No one was all bad. It might have been nice to see more of those positive traits over the years. Losing his grandfather had Eric thinking a lot about words left unsaid with families. He was more resolved than ever to call his brothers together before their father came home from the hospital. "Do you mind taking pictures of the papers and sending them over through text?"

"Not at all. Won't take long," Corbin said. "There are only five pages in here."

Eric remembered the file being thicker but maybe the Marshal only kept what he thought he could use later. "Send what you have."

"Will do," Corbin said. "Anything else while I'm in here?"

"That should do it," Eric said.

Corbin paused a few seconds. Then came, "Anything going on that I should know about, or can help with?"

"Nothing to share right now and you're already helping with what you're doing," Eric confirmed. His brother had questions. Of course, he would. This wasn't Eric's story to tell. He and Romy were off ranch property so the others shouldn't be in any danger. If the two of them were going back, he would have no choice but to warn the others. As it was, security knew what they needed to in order to keep an eye out. Kinkaid wouldn't go with a direct approach at the ranch anyway. He was trying to find a back door by using Romy and her sister.

Eric had to wonder how long it had taken for Kinkaid to

decide to use his own child as blackmail. Was he behind the entire threat?

He and Corbin said their goodbyes. Corbin made a special effort to tell Romy to be careful. The look that passed behind her eyes was all he needed to see to know how much she appreciated it. She deserved an army behind her, supporting her.

The phone buzzed multiple times in succession. The photos were coming through. Since he highly doubted Romy would let him study the small screen, he asked her to take a look at them first and describe the contents.

"This is probably going to take a couple of minutes," she said.

The fresh coffee warmed his throat and his head had stopped pounding. He was making progress on this thing. Slow, steady progress.

"Thank you for trusting me," he said to Romy while they waited. She could have simply spied on the ranch, given Kinkaid what he wanted, and then walked away. "You probably acted on impulse to tell me, but I appreciate it. This whole ordeal would knock anyone out of their comfort zone."

"My comfort zone definitely was obliterated the minute this whole ordeal started," she admitted. "Reaching back to the phone call with my sister that kicked it off. It's all happening so fast."

"Do you always take time to analyze every decision?" he asked.

"Yes. Except with my bakery. The timing didn't look right when I first looked at the possibility. There were two other bakeries that opened within a couple blocks of mine. I freaked out when I found out the second one had opened on the exact day I was supposed to put down a deposit on my space, along with the first month's rent. I had a couple of hours to decide to pull out or go for it," she admitted. There was a spark in her eyes when she talked about her business.

"The move clearly paid off," he said.

"Yeah. I guess I just decided on that day the business couldn't fail. Whatever else happened, I'd find a way to make it work, even if it meant outworking the competition or being more innovative," she said with that spark he loved. *Loved?*

Eric wasn't touching that thought with a ten-foot pole.

"Determination is a powerful thing," he agreed.

"It's so true. I decided ten percent of what happens to us is accidental and ninety percent is what we decide to do with it. You know?"

He did know. He smiled at her, thinking how attached he'd become to this woman in an incredibly short time and how difficult it would be to walk away from her.

16

"This is pretty condemning evidence if you ask me." Romy scanned documents which showed sketches of development on protected lands. Then, there was the transcript of the conversation Kinkaid had with Eric's grandfather stating getting permits wouldn't be an issue due to Kinkaid's relationship with the governor. She explained the contents of all five pages. "It's amazing what people say when they don't think anyone is listening."

"And how willing they are to tout an inappropriate relationship," he agreed.

"Boggles the mind," she said.

"The transcript would be inadmissible in court since it's illegal to record someone without their permission," he pointed out. "But there is enough here to threaten Kinkaid. Plus, he might not even remember what all he promised."

"At least your grandfather had the good sense not to go into business with the man." Romy figured the Marshal should get some brownie points there. Not that she was trying to defend a person she didn't know. In her experience, no one was all good or all bad. Most folks were shades of gray. In her case, for example, she'd learned over the years to focus on her mother's good qualities. Those helped soften the blow from the fact her mother didn't have a maternal gene in her body. Despite that, however, she had stuck around until Romy graduated high school and that couldn't have been easy.

"He loved Texas more than life itself. I'd like to think the Marshal's reasons were altruistic because he didn't want to partner with someone who was clearly doing dirty business. But, I think it had more to do with preserving Texas than doing the right thing. I've had to exit several business deals for him in recent years because I didn't trust his partners. He was starting to lose his edge in his older age and was doing some questionable things. It's part of the reason I decided to work the office end. I wanted to preserve his legacy and keep him on the straight and narrow as best I could. Make certain no one took advantage of him or sent him down a bad path."

"I understand. That was very kind of you to keep watch for him." She blew out a breath and returned to her spot on the bed next to Eric. "So, what's our next step?"

"I use what's on the phone to negotiate a trade," he said.

Her pulse kicked up a few notches. "I'm not good at playing poker, Eric. I don't waste money on slot machines. You know why?"

He shook his head.

"Because the games are always rigged to make you lose. Going all in with my sister's life on the line—"

"Is likely the only way to get her back in one piece," he stated. There was so much compassion in his voice. On some level, she realized he was right. Someone would contact her soon enough, and demand information on the Firebrands. What then?

Still, Romy didn't like any of this. "I wish we had more time to think this through."

"So do I," he said. "For many reasons." He gestured toward his head, and she assumed he meant that he also wished he had more time to heal, to be in top form physically and mentally. "But we don't. It's only a matter of time before they realize you're not going to send them anything they can use. Then what? Do you really think a man with a family and a reputation in the community is going to let your sister ruin that for him? The note he wrote in the card has been bugging me."

"Because it's the same song and dance from every person having an affair? A promise to leave their partner as the thing holding them back from going all in?" she asked.

"True. And true. But he pretended to be happy about the child and like he was convincing her it was a good idea to have the baby. Like she didn't want it," he said.

"She probably didn't. My sister has to know that having a child would be disastrous for her," Romy pointed out, her blood pressure on the rise. It always happened this way. Sasha would do something, and Romy would be the one to stress the most about it. Clearly, this was beyond anything that had happened in the past. This was far scarier than not being able to make rent. There was really no telling what other lies Kinkaid had told her. "What if he refuses the trade?"

"We figure out a different next step than the one I had planned," he said. "There's no perfect play here. We're going to have to take a risk in order to get your sister back in one piece."

"If anything happens to her, wouldn't his prints be all over her apartment?" she asked.

"A man like him would most likely have an excuse to

cover his tracks. But my guess is the altercation in her apartment might have been with someone sent to do Kinkaid's dirty work. Since he's the father and your sister said the blackmailer is threatening to expose the baby's dad, my guess is that he's playing both ends here. He must realize she wouldn't give him up," he reasoned. "He knows that he has her loyalty."

"If she's in love, she goes all in whether it's the smart choice or not," she said.

"Love has a way of making all logic go out the window," he said with a smile that practically melted the last bit of her resolve. For once in her life, she understood why and how a person would fall completely in love. Too bad she could never allow herself to let go because it would be with Eric Firebrand. Then again, it took two to tango and, other than a couple of sizzling kisses, the two of them hadn't exactly talked about the possibility of dating.

The circumstances were extreme. Emotions were heightened. What was happening between them couldn't last. It was too good to be true. The rug would be yanked from underneath her feet and she would be left alone, devastated.

Romy gave herself a mental headshake as she redirected her thoughts. No way could she afford to go down the road where she lost her heart to this man. Besides, right now, all she had time to focus on was Sasha.

"Kinkaid's personal cell is on one of the documents," Eric said. "We need to send him a text."

Romy took in a sharp breath and scanned the pages until she located the number. She grabbed the hotel pen and paper before scribbling the digits. "Here we go."

Eric dictated the text, and then told her which document to screenshot for the message. "Can you ask him to call immediately?"

Romy nodded. Her thumb hovered over the send arrow and for a split-second she wasn't sure she could go through with it.

"Take a deep breath and wait until you're absolutely ready," he said. "I can handle the conversation and I'll pretend like I found you out. You'll stay innocent in all this. It'll be best to protect you. I'll say you don't know that I'm contacting him."

"Okay." Her pulse thumped and her heart pounded. She took a few more seconds to gather her nerves before dropping her thumb.

The call was answered within seconds.

"WE CAN PLAY the game that I don't know what you asked my grandfather to do last year, or we can talk straight and start negotiating. Your choice." Eric didn't bother with formalities after saying who he was to start the call.

"I'm afraid you must have me confused wi—"

"Be strong, my angel," Eric recited the last line from the card. "Does that ring any bells?"

Kinkaid stammered on the other end of the line. "Doesn't change anything for me considering I have no idea what you're talking about."

"Really? Because I was going to swing by your house at 5555 Island Cove and drop off this lovely card with your wife. See what she has to say about whether or not this is your handwriting," he stated.

"Why would you do that?" Kinkaid's voice shook. He was breaking down just as Eric had hoped.

"Because Sasha doesn't deserve to be caught in the middle of your schemes and neither does the person you sent to spy on my family," he continued. "Using innocent people to do your dirty work doesn't sit well, Kinkaid. And I'm one hundred percent certain that the governor won't be able to get you out of this mess once this goes public. I'm also sure that he'll be on our side after a multi-year, multi-million-dollar campaign contribution.

Eric had no intention of structuring such a deal, but he would double up on the family's contribution to abused women's shelters. Kinkaid might not be physically abusing Sasha, but he was doing a number on the younger woman's mind and that deserved just as much attention.

"Well...I...this..." Kinkaid stammered.

The man was on the ropes, it was time to deliver the knockout punch.

"You can hem and haw all day, but you have ten minutes to get back to me with an exchange address. I'll bring the folder with all contents, along with my word I won't save anything on a device. You bring Sasha, safe and alive." Rather than wait for an answer, Eric ended the call.

His gaze immediately flew to Romy, praying she understood the tactic he'd taken.

She pushed off the bed and started pacing. "That was good. I think. He was nervous. I could hear it in his voice. And I realized that you had to finish strong but what if he goes for it and we show up without a file? Won't he want to see it before he makes the exchange?"

The last thing he would do was tell her to calm down, despite wanting to say just that. He'd played a big hand a few seconds ago and now it was time to find out if it would pay off. All the logical reasons Kinkaid wouldn't hurt Sasha flew out the window when fear and imagination took over.

"We'll stop off at the nearest CVS on our way over and buy a pack of manilla folders. Stuff a few sheets of paper in there that we dig out of the trash from the business center," he said.

"And what if he doesn't respond in the next ten minutes?"

The question hung in the air between them for a few short seconds before his cell buzzed. Romy practically dove onto the bed to check the screen.

"I know exactly where this is. It's where tourists line up to see the bats underneath the bridge," she said as a tear rolled down her cheek.

"Under the Congress Avenue Bridge," he confirmed. "What time?"

"Quarter after eight," she stated, and then locked gazes with him.

"Sunset."

"Yes. This is good, right?" she asked.

"It's progress," he said with a smile.

There would be a crowd. It would be easy to get lost. It would also be easy to send them into a trap. He would keep the last part to himself.

"It's half past eight." Romy's voice hovered at a notch below panic as Eric parked his mother's Mercedes on the street a few blocks from the bridge. Bright lights no longer blinded him after spending most of the afternoon in and out of sleep. There'd been pizza delivery for dinner while they reviewed the plan, part of which was being reasonably late.

"I know," he said, figuring a text would come in any minute now. Before he left the hotel, he'd messaged Kinkaid to come alone. He wouldn't. But his folks wouldn't hide in plain sight, which might give Eric the advantage he needed.

The evenings were still hot but nightlife in the live music capital of Texas thrived anyway. All walks of life crowded the streets and the bridge was no exception. The masses of people had given him the trick to his plan. Most folks would be walking away from the bridge after the show of bats. Kinkaid and his folks wouldn't be, making it easier to spot them.

Eric tucked the manilla folder under his arm before exiting the vehicle and making his way around to the passenger side. The rouse was up so there was no reason to leave Romy at the hotel. Plus, her quick thinking at the robbery might have saved their lives if things had gone sour. She'd been calm under pressure and he might need the assist, considering he was running at about seventy-five percent, maybe eighty. His confidence at this level of operation was high but it was always good to have backup.

Then there was the obvious move of her pretending that she was being forced into accompanying him. It would put her in the clear with Kinkaid if he believed she wasn't there of her own free will.

Romy gripped her cell phone, ready to make a quick 911 call should things go south. They were far more prepared this time, thanks in part to the robbery experience. Eric saw how vulnerable they'd been and had no plans for a repeat performance.

The hours in between the call and this meetup also gave Kinkaid a chance to prepare ahead of time. That part didn't qualify as warm and fuzzy.

They made the ten-minute walk from his spot near the Marriott, feeling a whole lot like salmon swimming upstream. The nightly bat show was over and smiling faces of couples and families passed by. The ear-to-ear smile on many of the kids' faces said the bats had been impressive.

Eric skimmed the faces as they passed by. If Kinkaid sent someone, the person would most likely be somewhere on the perimeter rather than in the main flow of traffic. Somewhere it would be easy to keep watch. Eric was hard to miss. He was tall even by Texas standards, which was an average of six-feet-tall. The bandage on the side of his head drew a couple of stares, mainly from curious kids. Adults glanced at him and then quickly looked away.

"There she is." Romy nudged Eric. There was a mix of excitement, relief, and fear in her voice.

"Kinkaid is with her. He's standing behind her," he said, noting that both of Sasha's hands were behind her back where he couldn't see them. Kinkaid also had her standing at the water's edge of the Colorado River. The current moved swiftly, and the water could be murky. At this time of night, it would be impossible to see anyway. "Tell me she knows how to swim."

"She's deathly afraid of drowning," Romy said.

Eric bit back a curse. He knew exactly what was about to happen and he didn't like any of it. In order to ensure Eric didn't follow Kinkaid, he planned to throw Sasha in the river. Eric would go to the drowning victim and Kinkaid would make his escape.

There were a couple of problems with Kinkaid's plan. First, Eric. This might be his first blackmail situation, but he was no stranger to dealing with criminals. Second, Eric had no plans to allow Romy or her sister to die tonight.

"Stop right there," Kinkaid warned.

"What are your swimming skills like?" Eric asked Romy out of the side of his mouth, keeping his voice low.

"I was a lifeguard every summer all four years of high school," she supplied.

"Are you okay with grabbing your sister if she goes in the water?" Eric kept his voice low.

"I'm solid," she reassured.

"Good. Because you might need to do just that. But not if I can help it," he said, wishing there was another way. A panicked swimmer wasn't someone he wanted Romy anywhere near. Survival instinct would kick in and Sasha could very well end up drowning Romy in the process of trying to save herself. An idea popped. "On second thought, hold up your cell phone where he can see it. Start recording."

Romy did.

"Go ahead," Eric urged as the two of them moved closer. "Toss her in the river."

From this distance, he could see Sasha trembling. He stopped Romy from getting any closer for fear she would lose it with Kinkaid. Eric wasn't ready to give up their rouse that she was only there because he was forcing her.

"I know you brought other people here tonight," Eric started. "So it should be no big surprise to you that I did the same."

His lie resonated with Kinkaid, whose eyes widened. His gaze shifted around like he was looking for the nearest escape route.

"What? I have, like, fifty brothers and cousins. You didn't think I'd bring backup?" Eric nodded to a dark spot on the other side of the river. He glanced over to their left and then nodded above. "Try anything stupid and not only will this video go viral, but Austin PD will be dredging your body out of this river come morning. Scuba teams can't work in the dark so you'll be long since dead by the time divers can jump in and look for you. But, hey, they'll have fun counting the bullet holes in you."

"How do you know I'm not doing the same thing? Recording this 'exchange?'" Kinkaid's shaky voice was a dead giveaway. He was like a kid who'd been caught red-handed but continued the lie anyway.

Eric didn't bother with a response.

"Let Sasha walk toward us. When she gets halfway here, I'll toss the file over," Eric stated with authority, bluffing his way through it. "We can be done with this whole ordeal in a matter of minutes."

Kinkaid shifted his weight from foot to foot as he continued to search for an alternate route. He seemed to realize his leverage no longer existed. "Fine. A deal is a deal. I hand over the girl for the file."

Nice of him to call his mistress a girl. Sick son-of-a...

Eric stopped himself right there.

"That's what we agreed to," Eric stated, meeting her halfway. As she passed by, she started to break down into tears. Her shoulders rocked as the first sob released and she ran the rest of the way toward her sister.

The move momentarily blocked Romy's camera. Kinkaid seized on the moment, pulling a gun on Eric. At this range, even a novice was guaranteed a hit. So, it was no shock to Eric when he felt fire shoot through his left elbow after a bullet split the air.

17

"Get down and stay down until I say different," Romy commanded her sister. Sasha was in shock and needed the jolt because a moment ago she'd stood there staring with a blank look on her face.

Romy put her hands on either side of Sasha's face. "Look at me."

Sasha did.

"I need you to do something for me right now," Romy continued, praying her sister could snap out of shock. "Follow me with my phone. Okay?"

Sasha nodded.

"You can do this. Right?" Romy asked, searching her sister's eyes.

"Yes," Sasha said with a headshake. Her gaze focused, giving Romy confidence Sasha was coming back.

As it was, Romy had no time to process that her sister was here, safe. All she could think about was getting to Eric and stopping a second shot from being fired. The first had caused her heart to stop beating for a few seconds.

Eric was on the ground, rolling around with Kinkaid.

For a long moment, she couldn't tell up from down when it came to the two of them. All she saw was blood on Eric's arm and clothes, and panic gripped her. Nothing could happen to this man. Period.

She was also smart enough not to get close enough for Kinkaid to drag her into the fight or somehow use her against Eric. And yet, she would do whatever it took if an opportunity presented itself.

From what she could tell, Eric was in control of the death roll the two were engaged in. In the next moment, a weapon went flying. It had to be Kinkaid's gun. It skidded past Romy and right into the hands of Sasha. Her sister's blank expression scared Romy more than anything else. She'd seen this once before that day when Sasha was in the hospital. Twelve years old. Defenseless.

"Stop," Sasha shouted, picking up the gun and aiming it directly at Eric and Kinkaid. "Or I'll shoot you both right now."

"Hold on there." Romy put her hands up, palms out, toward her sister. "Don't do anything you'll regret."

The men froze with Eric coming out on top.

"See, everything's all right now," Romy said as a guy came jogging toward them from behind Sasha, his gaze intent on her.

Before Romy could warn her sister, Sasha spun around, aimed, and fired.

The guy stopped cold as shock overtook his features and a red dot flowered on his white button down shirt. He sat down, bottom to pavement, with a dumbfounded look on his face. "She shot me."

Sasha turned back around, aiming the gun at Kinkaid this time.

"Sasha, no. Don't do it, sweetheart," Romy said.

"Give me one reason why not," Sasha said, her voice detached.

"The baby," Romy said.

"Is gone. He killed it." She pointed the bottom of the barrel at Kinkaid. Romy had no idea what happened but she needed to divert her sister's attention away from the pregnancy and the man responsible.

"Then, me," Romy said, desperate. "Don't shoot for me. Okay? We're going to get all of this worked out. I'll find the best counselors. You can come live with me, and we'll start a new business together. A nail salon like we talked about when you were a kid." Tears streaked Romy's cheeks despite her best efforts not to cry. "Just please don't shoot anymore."

At this point, a crowd was forming, and screams echoed across the river.

"He killed the baby and he was going to kill me next," she said, the blank expression was not a good sign.

"It was a miscarriage," Kinkaid shouted. "I didn't kill our child. I would never do that to you. I love you. We're going to build a life together. Remember?"

"You don't get to speak." Romy marched over and planted her foot in the man's jaw. She heard it snap when she fired off the second kick.

"I didn't want the baby and now it's gone. I didn't know how much I wanted it until it was gone," Sasha sank down to her knees, but her aim didn't waver.

"Look at me. Please. I'm here for you, Sasha. But if you shoot him there's no justice to be served. He gets off easy. As it is now, he'll spend the rest of his life behind bars for what he's done," Romy said. Her words seemed to penetrate the haze over Sasha's brain, a haze that caused her gaze to defocus and fear to rip through Romy. "Let's send him to jail, Sasha. He needs to pay for what he's done. Dying is the easy way out. This jerk needs to face the consequences of what he's done...what he's doing. Don't let him off easy, Sasha."

"Okay." Sasha released her grip on the gun, letting it dangle from her index finger.

Romy ran to her sister, kicking the weapon out of the way as cops arrived on the scene. Witnesses immediately pointed out Kinkaid.

"It's over," she said to her sister, pulling her against her chest. "It's going to be okay now. You're safe."

"I shot someone," Sasha said with a detached voice, dissolving into Romy's arms as the cops placed Kinkaid under arrest and EMTs attended to the wounded man who was sitting up, looking like he was in shock.

"He's going to be okay. We're going to get you the help you need, Sasha," Romy promised, and meant it. She wasn't in a rush to start a new business. Not yet. She needed to get her family straight. Sasha was all Romy had, and she had no plans to leave her sister to her own devices.

"Yeah?" Sasha asked, looking up at Romy with the purest brown eyes.

"I promise," Romy said. "I'm here. I'm not going anywhere. Let me help you."

"I lost the baby." Sasha sobbed.

Eric walked over, his undershirt wrapped around his elbow. "Do you live far from here?"

Romy shook her head.

"Mind if I stay at your place tonight?" he asked. "I can't imagine driving home right now."

"You're always welcome at my house," she said before glancing at his shirt. "But there's so much blood. Shouldn't you go to the hospital first?"

"And do what? Let them clean up a wound that I can take care of myself?" he asked.

"It looks serious," she continued, afraid he was more hurt than he wanted to admit.

"Believe it or not, I've had much worse." He cracked a small smile. At least his sense of humor was intact. That had to be a good sign.

She looked down at her sister, who'd dissolved in Romy's arms. "I have my hands full right now but there's a guest bedroom. You're welcome to it."

"I'd like that," he said, causing her heart to skip a beat. "Ready?"

"Yes," she said without question. "But we have to give our statements."

He nodded, then waited for Romy and Sasha to give their accounts of the night's events. The ordeal was over. Romy had her sister back. She couldn't ask for more. Could she? Because her heart wished Eric could stick around too. But that was impossible.

Tell that to the heart, she thought wistfully. Because it wanted him to stay longer than a night.

ERIC HELPED Romy bring her sister to his mother's vehicle. Romy took the backseat with Sasha after rattling off her address in the city. He found street parking, no small miracle, and helped both women out of the car. Sasha clung to her sister as he locked up, and they made their way inside the building and to the elevator.

The two-bedroom apartment with views of the capital was located in the center of town. The main room living space was open. A large granite island separated the kitchen from the living room. The room itself was good-sized with a wall of floor-to-ceiling windows. The décor was soft and the furnishings modern.

"Make yourself at home," Romy said to him.

"Mind if I make a cup of coffee?" he asked.

"Can you make that two?" she asked, motioning toward a cabinet. "I'll be out as soon as I get my sister showered and in bed."

"I don't need help, Romy," Sasha said before turning to wrap her arms around her sister's neck. "I know where everything is. You don't have to hold my hand."

"Are you sure that you're okay?" Romy asked.

Eric made arrangements to have their personal belongings sent over from the hotel before busying himself in the kitchen in an attempt to give the sisters some privacy, which was difficult to do in a small apartment. The coffee maker wasn't hard to find. It was on the counter. Making coffee wouldn't be difficult considering this one took pods, which were stored in a clear box underneath the machine. He refilled the water well. All he had left to do was find the mugs, which were in the cabinet Romy had motioned toward. He grabbed a pair before placing one under the spout. A minute later, he had two steaming cups ready to go.

As he turned around, Romy took a seat at the granite island. He handed over a steaming mug.

She rolled it around in her palms before taking a sip.

Eric took a couple of steps back and leaned against the counter behind him. The coffee was exactly the way he liked it...strong.

"We should take a look at your elbow," she said, bringing her gaze up to meet his. Electricity pulsed through him the minute their eyes made contact. There was something different. Something he couldn't quite pinpoint. Was it sadness? Desperation?

"It's fine," he said. "I'll clean it up in a few minutes."

Romy exhaled a slow breath. She glanced behind her as she lowered her voice and said, "She seems determined to make a change."

"Do you think she means it?" he asked.

"I do this time. In the past, she would have wanted me to take care of her. Not this time. She told me in the bathroom that she appreciated the offer to start a business but that she needed to get her head on straight first. Said that she's tired of letting her past hold her back and it's time to grow up and face the future." She took another sip of coffee. "She's never remotely said anything like that before."

"Maybe the pregnancy made her look at life differently," he said. He'd seen firsthand how different Adam was ever since he became a father.

"I hate what happened to her. The whole ordeal is awful and I can only imagine what she's been through. But she seems different. The old Sasha never would have picked up that gun. And if she did, she would have shot Kinkaid," Romy said. She involuntarily shivered at saying the man's name, and Eric wondered if she realized she'd done it.

"The mind is a powerful tool. Once it's made up, anything is possible," he said, realizing the heart worked the same way. Once it locked onto someone, it had no qualms about going all in. He was just beginning to realize just how much his had locked onto Romy. But then, he'd dated around. He wasn't a kid anymore. He knew what he wanted in life and in love...Romy.

Their chemistry was undeniable but did she feel the same way about creating something lasting?

And then she locked onto his gaze. Her expression turned serious. And his gut clenched. There was something serious on her mind.

"I'M NOT the type to rush into things, Eric. So, I hope you'll hear me out before you respond to what I have to say." Romy felt like her heart might burst if he walked out of that door tomorrow without knowing how much being with him had changed her life.

He nodded, his gaze hooded by thick lashes.

"I take my time and plan. I evaluate all the ins and outs before making a move. So, I'm completely out of my comfort zone here," Romy said as she held onto her coffee mug. Her heart threatened to break through her ribcage from the inside out. And yet, not saying what was on her mind would shatter her if she lost this man.

Staring into those beautiful eyes, one word came to mind...*home.*

"I don't want this to end," she continued, hoping to find the right words. When none came, she decided to say whatever came to mind. "Your birthday is October twenty-nineth, and your favorite color is blue."

"Like your eyes," he said, studying her.

"I may not know everything about you, but I know you." She had no idea if he felt the same way, but there was only one way to find out. "I've fallen hard for you, Eric. I'm ready to jump in with both feet and see where this takes us. What do you think? Am I way off base here?"

She took in a breath and held it while she waited for an answer.

"Just so you know," Eric started. "I'm in love with you. And if you think you could feel the same way, I hope to end up at the altar. I want to marry you and spend forever getting to know all your quirks and all the things that make you special. But if all this is too fast for you, then I'm a patient—"

She was already shaking her head as tears of joy streamed down her face and she let out the breath she'd been holding.

"Eric Firebrand. I'd marry you right here and now if it was legal," she said to him as he made his way around the granite island. At some point, he must have put his coffee cup down. Although, she had no idea when that happened. He looped his arms around her waist and hauled her against his chest, wincing in pain.

"Don't hurt your elbow," she said.

"It'll heal. Losing you would be a whole different story, Romy." He dipped his head down and claimed her lips, tender at first and then with bruising need.

When he pulled back, they were both out of breath. But when he looked into her eyes, she saw nothing but love. A love she wanted to grab hold of with both hands and never let go.

"A person like you comes around once in a lifetime, Eric. I want to grow old together," she said.

"Then, marry me," he said, dropping down on one knee. "Make me the happiest person on earth."

"Yes," she said, wiping away tears of joy. "I can't wait to be official, but my heart already belongs to you."

Romy finally found her spot, her home, and the place where she belonged. And she had no plans to let go.

18

Fallon Firebrand was back on Texas soil for the first time in fourteen years. He counted himself lucky to be coming home. A percentage of the men he served alongside who'd also earn the right to wear the coveted Trident insignia on every SEAL's uniform never got the same privilege. Being alive wasn't something he took for granted.

Word of his grandfather's death earlier in the summer had reached Fallon at a time when he was close enough to the end of his current contract to finish it out before requesting discharge. Thanks to the family's successful cattle ranch, he didn't need to stick around for a retirement package or worry about finances. He had a job waiting for him back home. One, he thought he'd have time to claim. The Marshal's sudden death had been a wake-up call. Time waited for no one.

Fallon was ready to lay claim to his birthright. He'd known this day would come. Still, it was strange being back on U.S. soil after all this time.

First things first, he needed to call his brother Eric to get the lay of the land. Eric picked up on the first ring.

"Now, this is a voice I haven't heard in too long," Eric said after initial greetings.

"I'm in San Antonio," Fallon admitted.

"What are you doing there?" Eric's voice had a reserved, calm quality.

"Coming home," Fallon said.

"For a visit?" Eric's interest seemed piqued.

"For good." Fallon had no idea how he fit into the family anymore. All he knew for certain was the timing was right.

"That's music to my ears," Eric said. Then added, "I'm guessing you received word about the Marshal."

"I did," Fallon said on a sharp sigh. "My contract was almost up, so I missed—"

"You don't need to explain yourself to me, man. You know that, right?" Eric's voice was reassuring.

"I do. Still can't help but feel like I should have been here before," Fallon said.

"I'm guessing you haven't heard about Dad," Eric said.

"No," Fallon said.

"He had a heart attack," Eric came right out with it. His brother's no-nonsense quality was exactly the reason Fallon had called him first. Eric was older by a couple of years, Fallon being the sixth of nine boys on their side of the family.

"What happened?" Fallon didn't bother to hide his shock.

"Long story," Eric said. "Are you sure you want to hear this right now? A lot has been happening at the ranch. Most of it is best told over a cold beer."

"As good as a long neck sounds right now, I'd better get the high level." Fallon figured he should have some idea what he was walking into. It was strange to think how much had changed over the years because in his mind, time had stopped at the ranch, no one had aged, and everything would look the same.

"Are you sitting down?" Eric asked.

"I bought a truck and I'm sitting in it. Why? There's worse than Dad having a heart attack?" Fallon asked. He shifted into Reverse and backed out of his parking spot, figuring he could get on the road while he finished this conversation.

"Adam is married with a kid," Eric said.

"Hold on...what?" Fallon didn't bother to hide his disbelief.

"You heard right the first time," Eric said with a chuckle.

"That is big news," Fallon agreed.

Another chuckle came through the line.

"Is there more?" Fallon's mind was already blown.

"Do you remember Raleigh Perry?" Eric asked.

"Of course. The guys overseas love her. The new song, *The Loft,* is probably some of her finest work," Fallon said.

"She's Raleigh Firebrand now," Eric said.

"Wait. What?" Fallon navigated off base.

"You're asking the wrong questions. You should be asking, 'Who?'" Eric stated.

"I have no guesses," Fallon admitted.

"Brax," Eric supplied. "And there's more about him but that's not a conversation we can have over the phone." Eric paused a beat. "Or maybe it is. It's the reason Mom left Dad."

"Lucia Firebrand left our father?" Fallon asked. How much could one family possibly change?

"Just for a few days because, it turns out, Brax was the product of an affair. His birth mother died during childbirth and our mother took him in as her own. Fudged his birth certificate to make him thirty-seven when he's actually thirty-six," Eric said.

"That's the same age as Corbin," Fallon said.

"Exactly," Eric agreed. "Do you remember Liv Holden?"

"Corbin's best friend?" Fallon asked.

"Yes. She married Kellan. Then, divorced him. And now she and Corbin are married," Eric continued.

"That must be causing a rift in the family," Fallon said.

"You have no idea," Eric confirmed.

"I always thought Liv and Corbin would make a great couple," Fallon pointed out.

"They do," Eric said before adding, "Dane's back."

"His twenty years isn't up," Fallon said. "I thought he wanted to go the distance."

"He medically boarded out," Eric said.

"Everything okay?" Fallon asked.

"There's nerve damage in his right hand," Eric said.

"It could be much worse," Fallon said on a sigh. He'd seen more than probably anyone should during his many tours.

"He's home and married now," Eric said.

"Is there something in the water at the ranch?" Something Fallon planned to avoid.

Eric laughed a little too loudly.

"Don't tell me you drank the water too," Fallon said.

"Her name is Romy," Eric said. "And we're about to get married in the back yard."

"Right now?" Fallon said. It was then he heard the music starting up in the background. "Guess that answers my question."

"I'm in love with her," Eric said. Now, Fallon understood the happy undertones in his brother's voice.

"Go make her your wife," Fallon said.

"Are you sure you don't want us to wait?" Eric stated.

"I'm a couple hours out. Don't put your plans on hold on my account," Fallon said. "Besides, I'll be there in time to raise a glass to you and your new bride."

"If you're sure," Eric said.

"I am." The last thing Fallon wanted to sit through was a wedding. At least theirs would be outdoors. The thought of putting on a suit made Fallon want to unbutton his shirt. Give himself room to breathe.

"Okay, then. Wish me luck," Eric said.

"You sound happy, Eric. You won't need luck," Fallon reassured.

"See you soon," Eric said.

"I'm on my way." Fallon ended the call after congratulating his brother. He was genuinely happy for Eric, and the others too. Marriage might not be Fallon's cup of tea but he would never try to stop others from doing it. To each his own, was Fallon's basic life philosophy.

Getting home in a hurry no longer held its appeal. Was he ready to face all the changes?

Did he really have a choice?

To find out if Fallon takes a bride, continue reading here.

ALSO BY BARB HAN

Cowboy Target

Cowboy Redemption

Cowboy Intrigue

Cowboy Ransom

Crisis: Cattle Barge

Sudden Setup

Endangered Heiress

Texas Grit

Kidnapped at Christmas

Murder and Mistletoe

Bulletproof Christmas

For more of Barb's books, visit www.BarbHan.com.

ABOUT THE AUTHOR

Barb Han is a USA TODAY and Publisher's Weekly Best-selling Author. Reviewers have called her books "heartfelt" and "exciting."

Barb lives in Texas—her true north—with her adventurous family, a poodle mix and a spunky rescue who is often referred to as a hot mess. She is the proud owner of too many books (if there is such a thing). When not writing, she can be found exploring Manhattan, on a mountain either hiking or skiing depending on the season, or swimming in her own backyard.

Sign up for Barb's newsletter at www.BarbHan.com.

Printed in Great Britain
by Amazon

69875072R00111